CONTENTS

ONE: Caught! 7
TWO: Curse of the Dragons 17
THREE: A Poor Choice 23
FOUR: Threats and More Threats 31
FIVE: The Haunt 39
SIX: The Mangrove Hideout 46
SEVEN: Punishment in the Parlor 57
EIGHT: A New Job 64
NINE: Wind or Weirdness? 75
TEN: Old Man Parker 87
ELEVEN: Broken Eggs and a Leaking Boat 95
TWELVE: Old Demon Rum 106
THIRTEEN: Billy Muldoo 118
FOURTEEN: Judgment Day 129
FIFTEEN: The Train 140
SIXTEEN: The Secret 154
SEVENTEEN: Too Close for Comfort 167
EIGHTEEN: Getting Down to Business 181
NINETEEN: Guillermo! 195
TWENTY: Promises 208

O N E

CAUGHT!

It was dark in the closet under the stairs. And hot. Thomas wiped his face on the sleeve of his good white shirt and wished he had made it to his secret hiding place down at the bay. He would have, if those two dumb girls hadn't tagged after him all morning!

He had finally escaped them by saying he was coming into the house for his jacket so he could walk them to the church.

That was a lie, of course. He meant to slip through the center hall and out the back door, to the oak grove in back of the house. He would stay there until everybody left for the wedding. Then he would run down to his hiding place in the mangrove thicket on the bay.

Nobody, not even his best friend Hal, knew about that hideout. Sometimes he went there when he wanted to think about the pirate treasure buried under his house. Of course, Hal knew about the treasure.

Just as Thomas reached the back door, he saw the girls sneaking around the corner of the house. They were giggling, as if they knew exactly what his plan was. Backing up, he jerked open the door of the closet under the stairway and shoved his way past the boxes and packages until he was at the very back. Now if someone opened the door, he couldn't be spotted.

The only problem was that he might die of the heat before everybody finally went on to the wedding.

"Thomas? Thomas, honey?" His mother was calling to him as she came down the stairs.

In another moment Thomas heard her speak to someone just outside the closet door. "Where's Thomas now? It's time we all went to church."

Then he heard the voice of his step-father-to-be calling him from out on the back porch. "Thomas? Hoo there, Thomas! Come a'running now, son."

Thomas scowled in the darkness. He vowed he wasn't coming a'running or a'walking. His mama could have Mr. Parker if she was determined to, but not Thomas. Not ever.

He leaned back and put his head against the wall. He felt sick in the stomach, partly from the heat and partly from knowing that his angry vow was one he'd find hard to keep. His mother was going to marry Mr. Parker today. He'd tried his best to talk her out of it, but she wouldn't listen. Mr. Parker was going to move into this house, and into his mother's bedroom.

Worst of all, Mr. Parker's two daughters, Pearl and Indigo, had already moved in. Their silly dresses and ribbons and dolls were in boxes in Thomas's old bedroom, waiting to be unpacked. His things were out in the loft over the kitchen where he would be staying from now on.

Under other circumstances he would have liked this fine. The cookhouse was separated from the main house by the back porch. After their cook Lucy cleaned up the supper dishes and went home, he would have the whole cookhouse to himself. He would be close to the food, and he could sneak Hal in and himself out whenever he took a notion.

More than once he'd begged his mother to let him move into the loft over the kitchen. She always said he had to wait until he was old enough, say about fifteen. Now, even though he'd just turned eleven, he was suddenly old enough. It was Mr. Parker who said he was.

Lucy nearly had a fit when his mother had told her. "You ought not to put that little child out here to sleep, Miss 'Livia."

"I'm not a little child!" Thomas had protested.

"You ain't big. Biggety maybe, but not big," Lucy had replied. "This here cookhouse no place for anybody, big or little, come night. I been telling you it got a haunt in it."

"Now, Lucy, that's just a lot of nonsense," his mother had said.

"No, ma'am. When I be here working late at night, I feel that ghost breathing on me. I hear it rattling my dishes when I'm trying to put them away and shaking the pots in the cupboard. It's that old sailor's ghost—

that's what it is. The old man buried his gold right where this house stands, then died 'fore he could get it back. Now he got to haunt this place to guard it, scared somebody else dig it up."

Thomas had tried. Ever since he and Hal had gotten big enough, they had been digging holes under the house. Nothing ever turned up except bleached-out seashells and broken pieces of Indian pottery.

They'd gotten tired of doing that lately, so they hadn't done any digging to speak of. But Thomas firmly believed the treasure was there. "It's not all nonsense," he had told his mama. "You know yourself that treasure is buried right under this house."

His mother had tossed her head. "I've heard the tale many times," she'd said crossly, "but that doesn't make it true, and I do not hold with any of that business about ghosts."

Thomas had responded with a shrug. His mother had no imagination. "I kind of believe the haunt's here," he'd said, "though I ain't seen it or heard it— yet."

He remembered his uneasiness after he'd said that and his hasty comments: "I ain't scared of it, though. I want to sleep in the loft. Away from those girls!" He'd started to add, "and Mr. Parker," but he didn't.

Now from deep in the closet, Thomas could hear Mr. Parker's girls hopping up and down in their fancy high-buttoned shoes, as if they were playing hopscotch or something.

"We know where he is! We know where he is!" they shouted.

Thomas scrunched up tight behind a box.

"He's hiding in the closet," Pearl said smugly. "He said he was coming for his jacket, but he told a fib. We saw him go into the closet when we ran up on the porch." Pearl sounded as happy as if somebody had given her candy.

Pearl, the youngest one, wasn't even nine yet. She had shiny blue eyes and light brown hair always tied with a big plaid bow and pulled skintight over her ears.

There was a little silence. The sweat poured down Thomas's face, but he was afraid to try to wipe it off.

The closet door was pulled open. Probably by one of those hateful girls. Thomas kept absolutely still.

His mother sighed and moved toward the door. Then he smelled her cologne. She must have put half a bottle on for the wedding. "Oh, I can't believe he's in there," she said anxiously. "He hasn't hidden in the closet since he was a little boy."

" 'Course he is," Pearl insisted. "Why doesn't some-one just push back there and find him?" Thomas heard a large box being shoved aside. A thin beam of light fell across the space just the other side of his feet.

Thomas was so angry with Pearl he thought the hot skin of his face might split open. He was angrier at her than he was afraid of being found.

The light from the door was suddenly blotted out. Lucy spoke with authority. "Get yourself out of that closet, Miss Pearl. You're fixing to get your fine new dress all dirty." Thomas heard a little scuffle, and then the closet door slammed shut. He breathed a small sigh of relief in the almost airless dark.

Lucy's voice carried plainly into the deep of the closet. "Now you folks better get on down to the church. You want to be late to your own wedding? Forget about that Thomas. He's probably run on ahead to get him a back seat."

"But he's supposed to sit up front with the family," Thomas's mother protested.

"Don't hold him to that, Miss 'Livia. Boys don't take much to weddings. Let him sit in the back with me if he takes a notion."

"Well, I guess that would be all right," his mother said after a moment, not too happy about it. Then she quickly added, "Come on, girls. Come, Albert, dear. Let's do go on to church."

Thomas listened to their footsteps going down the hall to the front door. He was trying to decide if it was all right to crawl out of the closet when the door was yanked open again.

"You! Thomas! Quit your foolishness now and come out of there. We've got to get to the church quick as rabbits!"

Thomas scrambled out, feeling safe with Lucy's wide form filling the back of the hall. "But I'm not going to that old wedding."

" 'Course you're going. And right now. Here's your jacket—and the brush to slick down your hair."

"But I don't want to go!"

"That don't matter. This is something you *got* to do. Now come on. You made us both late."

Lucy's round face shone with sweat as they walked

down the sandy streets to the Methodist church at Five Points. On the church steps she wiped off her face with a huge white handkerchief and took Thomas's arm.

"Thomas, you love your ma, don't you?"

" 'Course I do," he whispered fiercely.

"Then just 'cause you love her, and never minding nobody else, why don't you walk on down that aisle and sit with the family?"

He groaned. "I can't. It's late, and everybody will stare at me."

"That won't matter. You just think about your ma seeing you and how good she's going to feel."

"Ohhh, Lucy . . ." He turned then, fixed his eyes on the narrow strip of carpet running down the center aisle, and took one step. He shot one last glare back at Lucy and whispered, "But I ain't sitting by those dumb girls!"

Thomas squeezed into a narrow space on the aisle by Great-aunt Lena Tisdale. They were not very fond of each other, but it was the only place he could sit without crossing over a lot of knees.

She examined him up and down and then sniffed as if he smelled bad or something. "You look a sight," she said.

He shrugged, thinking that she didn't look like much herself. She sure smelled. Like lilac cologne and vinegar. The vinegar was from the liniment she said cured her rheumatism.

She had on her dark purple taffeta dress with all the pleats and buttons and a hat big enough to shade a pair of hound dogs from the sun. She was fanning herself with her Chinese fan.

Thomas would have given anything to have that fan. It was made of dark red silk, with gold flowers and dragons painted on the silk. The ivory handles were carved in the shape of snorting dragons.

The fan was connected with the treasure buried under his house. Thomas knew this because his aunt had told him so a few dozen times. What she hadn't done was let him hold the fan to examine the dragons.

He had thought more than once of sneaking into her house and secretly studying the fan. Maybe it held a key to the exact location of the treasure! But his aunt could be something of a dragon herself, and he hadn't dared.

Thomas heard a stirring at the door of the church and knew his mother and Mr. Parker were getting ready to walk down the aisle. Hal's father, Preacher Watson, stood up ready to hear their vows.

Thomas heard them when the wedding guests murmured as they walked by. Just when they came even with him, his mother reached out, touched his arm, and walked on.

Thomas thought in that moment he was really going to disgrace himself. He was going to burst out crying right in front of everybody. He held himself rigid and gulped hard. Then he ducked his head down so he couldn't see his beautiful mother standing in front of the preacher near Mr. Parker. A little shudder went through his body that he couldn't control.

His Aunt Lena nudged him sharply. Then she

reached over and thrust her fan between his clenched fingers. He opened it gratefully and stared in amazement at the intricately carved dragons stretched along its handles.

A half hour later Thomas stood in his front yard staring down the long wooden table spread with the wedding feast. If there was anything at all good about the wedding, this was it.

With loaded plate he turned to see Mr. Parker motioning him to sit with his mother and him. He pretended not to see him and sat quickly at another of the small tables under the trees.

Immediately Pearl slid in beside him. "Ah-ha, Tommy-wommy, you're a sissy. We saw you playing with your aunt's fan."

Indigo sat down on the other side of him. Now he was trapped.

"Now you've gone and ruint my good dinner," he said. "Why'd you have to come and sit here?"

"We didn't come because we wanted to sit by you," Indigo said. "We came to tell you we saw you playing with the fan."

Thomas stared at Indigo, and she stared back, her eyes as dark brown as an Indian's, her thin red lips curved in a teasing smile. Her thick hair, braided in two pigtails down her back, was the same dark color as Thomas's, and he didn't like that at all.

"Why are you so much darker than your pa?" Thomas blurted out, thinking how much lighter skinned Mr. Parker was.

"What?" Indigo asked in surprise. Then collecting

herself, she said, "Oh, that. I just take after my mother. Her skin was olive and I just take after her." Then turning back to the subject of the fan, she repeated her earlier comment. "We saw you playing with the fan."

"I wasn't playing with no fan," he said indignantly. "I was looking at the dragons carved on it."

The girls' taunts suddenly inspired him to spin them a tale that would make them shake in their buttoned-up shoes.

"Listen," he said. "That ain't no ordinary fan, you know." He got up close to their faces and dropped his voice to a near whisper. "It's got an evil curse on it. Evil, evil. You brave enough to hear this?"

T W O

CURSE OF THE DRAGONS

Pearl had stepped behind Indigo, but Indigo held her ground, looking at him scornfully.

Thomas knew he had to come up with something really scary. He plunged in, making his tale up as he went along.

"This fan was made by a Chinese artist a long time ago. He painted the silk and carved the dragons. While he was finishing it, the captain of a Chinese pirate junk came up behind him and thrust him through with a big sharp sword!"

Thomas drove an imaginary blade down in front of Indigo's face. She blinked but didn't move. Thomas warmed to his subject and continued on. "Then he stole the fan and left the poor old carver drowning in his own blood."

The girls were staring, wide eyed. Thomas paused,

savoring their obvious interest. "And while this poor old man lay dying, he put a spell on the fan, a very evil one, and on whoever else owned the accursed thing!"

"Oh, really?" Indigo said after a moment. "What about your Aunt Lena?"

Thomas looked at her in disgust and then picked up a piece of sweet potato pie and took a bite out of it. He stared up into the spreading oak shading the table and most of his front yard. Well, what about his Aunt Lena? He could say, "Look how ugly she turned out," but that wasn't good enough.

"You don't understand the spell," he said. "What has to happen is that someone has to rub hard on the fan's handles, right on those dragons. Now if he has a good heart, he can throw the curse on somebody else. And if he has an evil heart, the curse comes back on him."

He took a deep drink of his lemonade and frowned at its sourness after the sweet-tasting pie. "And, you have to admit, my Aunt Lena may be homely and bossy, but you can't say she has an evil heart."

"And just how do you know all this?" Pearl asked.

Thomas didn't know any of it, for he'd made it up. But there was some other stuff about the fan that was true, some important stuff. He hadn't really planned to tell them about the treasure. It was something special about his house he hadn't planned to share with these dumb girls. But they were listening so well he couldn't stop himself from giving them the full story.

He wiped his mouth with the back of his hand. "I know a lot more. I know how my aunt got the fan."

"How?" Indigo looked as if she hated to ask, but couldn't stand not to know.

"My grandfather told me all about it, and something more important. He bought this land to build my mother and father a house for a wedding present. When the house was halfway finished, this old Chinese sailor came up in the yard fussing and cussing, mad as all get out. He said he'd buried something on this property and nobody had any business building anything on top of it. My grandfather thought he was probably crazy and that the easiest way to get rid of him was to let him dig under the house for whatever he had buried.

"The man fooled around under the house for a long time and then came out madder than ever. He had the dragon fan in his hand. He waved it at my grandfather and accused him of taking the rest of the treasure."

"What rest of the treasure?" the girls asked together.

"Give me time, will you? I'm getting to it. The sailor had gotten scared of the curse on the fan, you see." Thomas added that bit of his own imagination to his grandfather's story. "And he said he buried it in a red-lacquered box. But, and here's the best part, he also buried some gold pieces. They were the real treasure."

Indigo breathed out a sigh. "Humph. And so?"

Thomas shrugged. "Grandpa didn't like being yelled at, and he told the man to get off the property and never come back."

"And did he come back?" Indigo asked.

"I hope not," Pearl said. She looked around the yard apprehensively.

"Yes, he came back, two or three times," Thomas replied. "Once another man came with him, a big, black-haired Spanish sailor." He waited to be sure they were really listening before giving them the final details he hoped would finish them off. He leaned toward them and said, almost in a whisper, "But the last time he came, something really bad happened. He got bit by a *rattlesnake* about six feet long."

"Oh, my goodness sakes," Pearl said, clutching at Indigo.

"What happened then?" Indigo asked, looking as much interested as afraid.

"He took off running before the workmen could try to help him. Folks say he died down on the dock. The black-headed sailor cut his leg open and tried to suck out the venom, but he died anyway." Thomas paused. "Lucy says his ghost haunts the cookhouse."

Even Indigo looked impressed for a moment. She stared at him and then asked, "And the fan? You were going to say how your aunt got the fan."

"Oh, that. Well, that first time when he was so mad, he threw the fan at my grandfather and yelled, 'You take this blasted, accursed fan! You deserve its evil curse for stealing my treasure!'" He shrugged. "Grandpa didn't believe in such things as that, and he gave Aunt Lena the fan."

"But your grandfather hadn't stolen the treasure?" Indigo asked.

"Of course not, you ninny. Do you think my grandfather was a thief?"

"Did anybody else dig for it? After the sailor died?"

"Of course, lots of people. Me and Hal dug a million times, and we're still digging."

"Can I try?"

Thomas was alarmed by this development. "Of course not. Girls don't do things like that. Besides, do you think I'd let you mess around with my treasure?"

Indigo looked him straight in the eye. "What I think is that there's not a word of truth in anything you've said."

"Yeah, you're a fibber," Pearl said, a little less sure. "Just like folks say."

"You better hope I'm a fibber," Thomas said, angry with them now. "Because while I was holding that fan, I rubbed on the dragons." He pushed up from the table and, leaning over, hissed at them. "And I wished a curse on *you two!*"

"Fibber, fibber," Pearl said, putting her hands over her ears.

"Liar is more like it," Indigo said.

Pearl gasped. "We're not allowed to say that word."

"It's the only way to describe a boy like Thomas. And he *is* lying. That means even if there is a curse, it's going back on him. Nothing bad has happened to us, has it?"

Thomas picked up his plate. He was still hungry, and he wasn't going to let these silly girls ruin this wedding dinner for him. "Just you watch out. Before long, you'll begin to notice the signs."

"What signs?" they asked together.

Thomas tried to take his mind off the serving table still loaded down with Lucy's wonderful food. A small movement caught his eye. It was a brown-striped lizard skittering for cover under the bench.

"There are all kinds of signs," he said, "but the main one is lizards. They're like tiny dragons, you know. When you notice lizards all around you, you'd better watch out."

"That's silly," Indigo said. "In Florida, lizards are all around everyone."

"This is different," Thomas said. "They're not only around you, but they begin giving you the evil eye. You just watch. Next time you see a bunch of lizards, notice their eyes."

He ran before they could say another word, and he didn't get any more food. He had, purely by accident, set himself up for some real fun.

T H R E E

A POOR CHOICE

Thomas looked out over the wedding guests beginning to gather themselves to watch the cake cutting. Hal Watson was still eating at one end of a table.

"Quick, Hal," Thomas said, coming up behind him. "I need you to help me with something."

"I'm still eating. Besides, how come you sat with those girls instead of me?"

"I didn't sit with them. They ganged up on me. Anyway, come on. I've got a great idea to fix those two up good. Let's go to the grove back of the house, and I'll tell you what we're going to do."

They ran behind the house without being noticed, not even by Pearl and Indigo, who had gone over to watch the cake cutting.

"We got to pick up as many lizards as we can catch,

Hal, and in a hurry! Put them in your pockets and shirt."

"What for, for Pete's sake?"

"We're going to turn 'em loose in my bedroom—my old bedroom."

"But that's where the girls are staying," Hal said. Then his face crinkled up in a grin, and he dropped to his knees in the sand grabbing for a large black lizard.

Thomas grinned back. "When those girls go up to change their clothes, I want them to have lots of little creepy things for company. There's more to it, but I haven't got time to tell you now."

A few minutes later, Thomas and Hal ambled back around the house to rejoin the wedding party. They helped themselves to the golden wedding cake, covered with thick white icing and fresh coconut. They took cups of punch with ice brought from Mr. Parker's ice locker at the grocery store.

When anyone spoke to them, they answered very politely, even when it was an adult saying something dumb to Thomas like, "It's very nice for you to have a new papa, isn't it?"

Thomas hadn't thought much about his mother and Mr. Parker in the last half hour while he was eating and fooling with the lizards. Now the whole thing came back to him like a heavy weight in his chest. His whole life was going to be different and terrible, beginning with these next three days.

His mother and Mr. Parker were going to catch the steamer down at the pier and go off to Tampa on a honeymoon. Mr. Parker had scraped up the four dollars for the round trip. Thomas wished he'd scraped a little harder so he could take the girls. One way! No such luck.

Not only were the girls going to be here, his Aunt Lena would be sleeping on the divan in the sitting room. It was an awful arrangement.

Thomas put his cake on a table and sat down on the bench with his chin on his hand. Since his mother was determined to remarry, she could have at least picked out somebody decent—like a rancher from over by the Myakka River, or even good old Billy Muldoo.

Billy Muldoo lived on Sarasota Key across the bay from the mainland. He almost never came to town, and Thomas had never seen him close up. By all accounts Billy didn't work except to fish and to smoke or to dry the fish. He never had to take a bath or trim his beard. He never had to do anything he didn't want to do. He was free as any seagull. It seemed to Thomas the perfect kind of life.

Mr. Parker was just the opposite. He'd moved to Sarasota from Massachusetts about a year ago and set up a grocery and dry goods store on Main Street.

He was tall and thin with dark hair and eyes. Even though he had olive skin, he wasn't tanned brown as leather like most of the men around here. Mr. Parker didn't go hunting or fishing. He seldom left his store except to take in a delivery at the back door.

At first he hadn't been especially friendly to Thomas and Hal when they'd gone into the store on errands for their parents or to spend an occasional penny for candy.

Things had changed when Mr. Parker and Thomas's mother had started looking at each other with sheep's eyes. Mr. Parker began smiling at Thomas and trying to start up a conversation with him whenever he went to the store. Once Mr. Parker even offered him a piece of rock candy. Thomas took it to be polite, but after that he never went into the store at all if he could help it.

Thomas couldn't imagine how his mother could even like Mr. Parker, much less want to marry him.

"Hey, Thomas, I'm going back for more cake," Hal said, interrupting his thoughts.

Thomas didn't answer. He looked at the cake in front of him with disgust. Then, picking up the plate, he dumped the cake on the ground for the ants.

Everybody was watching his mother and Mr. Parker getting ready to leave. The girls were pulling at their father's arms, and his aunt was giving his mother a kiss on the cheek.

Ugh. His aunt and those girls. He was not going to stay in the house with that crowd for three days. Nobody could make him. He could slip into the kitchen now and fill his pockets with biscuits and chicken. No one would notice him cutting through the woods. He could hide out as long as he pleased in the mangrove thicket.

Thomas started toward the house and then stopped. He just couldn't leave until after the girls met up with those lizards.

Suddenly Thomas's mother came running over to

him with her arms wide. She seemed so happy it made him angry. But when she gave him a hug and a long kiss on the cheek, he felt her tears on his face and he couldn't be angry with her anymore.

"You will be good, Thomas, honey?"

"Yes, ma'am."

"And be kind to your new sisters?"

"They're not my sisters."

The tears started in her eyes again, and he added, "But I'll be kind as possible." He knew he couldn't tell her the truth, which was that he didn't plan to be around the girls at all.

She sank down on the bench by him. "Thomas, I know you're very unhappy now. But I'm hoping, and praying too, that in time you'll see how good this is for all of us. Especially for me. You're growing up and someday you'll go off and I'll be alone."

"You'll have Lucy."

She smiled. "She won't be enough. And Thomas, Mr. Parker is a good man, one you can love and respect. He wants to be a real father to you."

Thomas wanted to say, "He'll never be my real father," but the look on his mother's face stopped him. He busied himself scuffing his toes in the soft gray sand.

"Come along, Olivia, my dear," Mr. Parker said.

Thomas's mother looked up at her new husband with her face all full of smiles again. Thomas felt betrayed. Before she could turn back to him, he had jumped up and backed away from the bench.

Mr. Parker caught her hand, and they started running toward the carriage waiting to take them to the pier.

"Wait, wait, wait!" Pearl screamed after them, and they stopped. "We forgot to give you the presents we made for you."

She and Indigo started running toward the house, and Indigo called back over her shoulder. "They're up in our bedroom. We'll be right back."

Mr. Parker took out his gold watch to check the time. "We don't want to miss the steamer," he said.

"I'm sure the girls will be right back," Thomas's mother said. "How sweet of them to make us gifts."

Thomas held his breath and stared at Hal, who seemed to be holding his, too. They dared not move a muscle.

About the time Thomas thought he would pop, two blood-curdling screams pierced the hot spring air. The screams traveled down the stairs and out across the porch into the yard as Pearl and Indigo ran out of the house fluttering like chickens with their heads cut off.

Mr. Parker moved to catch them in his arms. "What on earth is the matter? Stop that screaming right now!"

"The curse, the curse," Pearl wailed.

"Hush now, hush. You're not acting like little ladies at all."

Aunt Lena stepped forward. "Now, don't worry, Mr. Parker. They're just overwrought with the excitement. I'll take care of them. You all go on and catch your boat."

She moved heavily in all her purple glory toward the two girls. "My goodness, you've worked yourselves into a state. Here, let me fan you."

Pearl took one look at the carved ivory fan moving her way and dropped to the ground in a dead faint.

There was a whole lot of confusion for a few minutes. Thomas poised himself to run. He could get away right now without being noticed. Just then Hal latched onto his arm, snickering under his breath.

"You want to run away to Cuba?" Thomas whispered.

"Heck, no. I wouldn't miss the rest of this for the world."

"Hah. When the girls get a chance, they're going to tell, and we're both going to be in bad trouble. Your father will lick you for sure."

"It's worth it."

Mr. Parker had picked up Pearl and was holding her while Thomas's mother patted her cheeks and called her name.

Pearl's eyes opened, and Lucy stepped forward. She took Pearl out of her father's arms. "She's gonna be all right now. Poor little thing. The heat got her. I'll take her in and wash her down with cool well water. Miss Indigo, you come on, too. You need to rest yourself a spell in your room."

"No, I don't," Indigo said. "I'm never going back in that room! It's full of lizards with beady eyes. They stared at us."

Mr. Parker looked at his watch again, then shook his head and began guiding Thomas's mother toward the carriage. "We have to go," he said. "That's all there is to it."

He turned and concentrated a look on Thomas. What his eyes were saying to Thomas was "You and I will deal with this properly when I get back."

He looked just like a real father. A very cross one.

FOUR

THREATS AND
MORE THREATS

As soon as his mother was out of sight, Thomas tried to locate Hal. He didn't have to look far. Hal was standing by the serving table with a ham biscuit in one hand and a piece of fried chicken in the other.

When Thomas whistled at him, Hal made his way over, chewing happily as he came. His red hair stood out at angles in the breeze, and his Sunday clothes looked as if he had been somewhere besides in Sunday school.

Thomas's own wool suit was wet with sweat. His wide white collar, which Lucy had ironed stiff with starch, was now limp at his neck. He loosened the plaid bow under his chin and wished again he could grow out of these baby clothes. Even more than the bow, he hated his pants hanging just below his knees with the awful brass buttons on the hems. If he was old enough to sleep in the loft, he ought to be old enough to wear a man's long pants and tie.

"What now?" Hal asked.

"I was just thinking about shucking these plagued wedding clothes and going swimming. How about going skinny-dipping right down there in the bay?"

Thomas knew this wasn't a good idea, but right this minute he really wanted to do something on the bad side.

Hal was staring at him wide-eyed. "With those girls and the rest of the wedding party and your Aunt Lena right here in the yard? You're crazy!"

"I dare you. I double dog dare you."

Hal sent his chicken bone sailing through the air. Thomas's old pet, Coon Dog, had been watching them from under the table. Now he crawled out and loped over to retrieve the bone.

"All right, Thomas, my boy. You got yourself a dare. Let's get out of these monkey clothes, and put on our overalls for after. I'll meet you at the big cedar." With that, Hal turned and trotted off through the yard.

Thomas, already sorry he'd thrown out the dare, walked slowly along the side of his house and over the back porch into the kitchen. Lucy was there cleaning up. Her grandson Sample was stacking clean plates in a cupboard.

Sample usually came to help her when she had to work after dark, because she feared the haunt. Fortunately, Sample didn't care about haunts. Thomas thought for a minute about asking him to stay the night, but decided against it. *After all, I'm not scared of haunts either, am I?* he concluded.

Sample was Thomas's age and one of his best fishing buddies. "Hey, Sample! You just get here?" Thomas asked in a hurry.

Sample grinned. "Yeah, I missed all the big doings. I been over to the railroad to see about getting me a job."

Thomas was impressed. As far as he was concerned, the biggest doings in Sarasota had to do with the railroad tracks being laid right in town. "Well, ain't you something now," he said. "Did you get yourself a job?"

Sample grinned again and ducked his head. "Yep. I'm going to be one of the main water boys."

"Oh." That didn't sound too great, but it was better than nothing. "How long you reckon before the train is going to come into town?"

Sample shrugged. "I don't know about that. I just know they laying ties fast as the grading crews even out the sand."

Lucy shoved a wooden bucket into his hands. "You such a good water boy. Now get your grandma a bucketful."

She turned to Thomas. "It's time you showed up in this kitchen, mister smarty pants. I thought maybe the marshal caught up with you. Where's that Hal?"

"Gone home. I'm gonna meet him down at the bay in a few minutes and go swimming."

"Not now you ain't. Not till you undo some of your

mischief. Them poor little girls is sitting in the parlor upset as two wet hens. I sent for their old cook Hattie Mae to stay with them tonight. They ain't having no part of Miss Lena." She stopped and put her hands on her big hips. "Somehow you is mixed up in that, too."

Thomas threw out his hands innocently. "Who? Me? I don't have much to do with Aunt Lena myself. Those girls are just silly gooses, that's all. I hate 'em. I hate both of them!"

"Hush up that kind of talk. They's your sisters now. Nobody can make you love them, but you sure got to live with them. And you can't hate them either. God don't like that hating business."

"Why did God make girls, anyway?"

"So boys can get born into this world, for one thing. I don't want no more talk now. You find Hal and you get upstairs and get all them lizards together and out of this house."

"Lizards! What lizards?"

"You know mighty well what lizards, and I want them out of here right now. With all else I got to do already, now I got to go up and make a pallet for Hattie Mae. I sure don't want no lizard running over her tonight. Her screams'll stir up the dead at the cemetery."

Thomas thought immediately that he'd have to leave a couple of lizards in the bedroom.

Lucy caught his arm as if she'd read his mind. "And if she screams, you're going to wish you was dead and in the cemetery yourself. You hear me?"

"I hear you. Hattie Mae hadn't got nothing on your

mouth, you know." He pulled away and ran out of the house to find Hal. This really wasn't such a good time to go skinny-dipping.

A half hour later Thomas crawled on his hands and knees out from under the high wooden headboard of the bed. As far as he knew, he had every one of the lizards in the hatbox Lucy had given him to put them in. Hal had refused to help.

Thomas looked up when Indigo stepped inside the door. "I'll get you for what you did," she said. "I'll play a trick on you you won't forget. And I'm going to tell on you, too."

"Tattletale, tattletale, hang your britches on a nail." Thomas picked up the box and rattled it at her.

Indigo backed up a step, but she didn't scream or run away. "I'm not really afraid of those dumb things. You just got me scared a little bit with that lie about the fan."

"Well, you don't know for sure that it was a lie, do you? And you don't know all of it either. Just wait till you hear the ghost one night."

"I suppose you've heard it."

"Lots of times." This was mostly a lie. He'd never for sure heard the ghost, even when he and Hal used to dig under the house.

Indigo had looked briefly into any attention to shrugged. "I'm just not going to get out of you. My father said understands things like that." said to expect, why is he running a plain old My fa grocery store? He doesn't even own a house either, and you all moved in here on me and my mother."

Indigo turned a little pale under her tanned skin, but she stood her ground. "My father was going to buy a house. We had one in Massachusetts before we moved down here. But your mother wanted to keep this house. She said your grandfather built it for your father. It was your home, and she wants to keep it for you. And my father was kind and agreed that she could."

Kind? Mr. Parker kind? Thomas had only seen him serious at the store—weighing things out just so, scolding the boy who worked for him if he didn't sweep the corners clean or deliver the groceries fast enough.

"He's kind," Indigo went on. "He speaks very sternly, but that's just his way. And he wants to do his best for you. He said so. When he comes back, he's going to put you to work at the store."

Thomas sat down on the floor again and stared at her. "Me? Work at your father's store?"

"Yes. I heard my father tell your mother you need a man's firm hand to straighten you out. You need hard work to do so you won't get into mischief all the time." The tall, black got up slowly now. He was very angry. This even like was Mr. Parker whom Thomas didn't mother, who at to try to run his life. And his either, was apparent at Thomas didn't like much

"You're some kind of let him do it!

ing past her. In the hall he said, stalk-

"And you'll

36

never get even with me. Never. For every trick you think up, I've got ten planned ahead of you." He pointed past her to the hatbox from which the sound of small scrambling feet could be heard. "And since you're not scared of lizards, you take that out and empty it!"

Thomas ran down the steps, thinking he would get away from the house right away. He didn't want to spend one more minute here alone with the girls and his Aunt Lena. He started out the back door to go to the kitchen when he heard Lucy in there banging things around, the way she did when she was in no mood for conversation.

She wouldn't take kindly to his coming in and packing up some food. If he took any large amount, it would certainly make her suspicious. He would just have to wait around until she had finished her work and gone home.

"Shucks! And consarn it, too," he said under his breath. He would like to shout the words out loud, but no use asking for more trouble right now.

His Aunt Lena appeared suddenly in the doorway of the sitting room. "What are you muttering about, young man? Did I hear you say a bad word?"

"Me? A bad word?"

"Humph. I should hope n̶o̶t̶ ... the little girls. We're going ... at tonight. That ought to Then w... portmanteau."

Thomas groaned. "Aunt Lena, do I have to?"

She fixed him with a very cross stare. "Don't you want to be helpful?"

"I don't mind carrying your suitcase, but the girls? Do I have to look at pictures with the girls?"

"Yes, you do," she snapped. "No more argument now. Find your stepsisters."

FIVE
THE HAUNT

The loft was absolutely dark and very quiet. Not even a mouse ran across the rafters above Thomas's head. When he moved, the straw ticking of his pallet made crunchy sounds that, in the silent darkness, sounded awfully loud.

Thomas wondered why he had ever thought it would be fun to sleep up here. More than that, he wondered if there really was a ghost haunting the cookhouse.

He should have asked Sample to spend the night. Sample wasn't afraid of the ghost. And neither was he! His grandfather had said if you died and went to heaven, you wouldn't want to come back; and if you died and went to hell, the devil wouldn't let you come back. That ought to take care of the old sailor's ghost.

No matter what else, Thomas was near the food.

He sat up on the pallet. He still felt pretty hungry. The small supper at Aunt Lena's really had been small— nothing but a bowl of clabber and bread with scuppernong grape jelly.

There'd been no time to get anything else to eat since then. They'd all looked at those dumb pictures of Aunt Lena's for what seemed like hours. Finally, Hattie Mae had come to take the girls off to bed.

Thomas thought then he was free at last, but his aunt, like some kind of fierce guardian angel, had walked him to the kitchen, carrying the kerosene lamp, and had stood there watching until he had climbed the ladder up into the loft.

He didn't know what time it was now, but he did know he was hungry. Cautiously, he crawled along the floor and at the edge of the loft stopped to stare down into the kitchen.

A small amount of light from a three-quarter moon came through the kitchen window, and he could see the pie cabinet in the corner. He'd find bread and pie there, for sure.

It was dead quiet in the kitchen. The scrubbed wooden table looked so different in the daytime with Lucy pounding dough or chopping chicken on it.

Doggone that Lucy! he thought. *She's just put an unnatural fear in me. That's what she's done.*

He took another long look around the darkened kitchen, then turned around and began to go slowly down the stairs. He stalled in the middle, listening. If there were a ghost, he was a quiet one.

Hitching up his long nightshirt, he slowly reached

out a foot to find the next step. Then he froze against the ladder.

A wet and icy hand had suddenly closed tightly around his ankle. For a moment he couldn't even breathe. Then jerking his foot free from the hand, he made it back up to the edge of the loft in nothing flat. He squatted there shivering, staring down into the kitchen.

There was nothing or nobody there. The kitchen was absolutely empty and quiet. The shutters were in place across the window, and the door to the porch was shut.

Maybe I imagined the cold, wet hand, he thought hopefully. He drew up his foot and looked at it, then felt his ankle. It was damp all right. And it still felt cold. He hadn't imagined it. He couldn't have.

He wished again for Hal or Sample. He wouldn't be scared at all with either of them here.

They weren't here, but old Coon Dog was.

Thomas gingerly tackled the ladder again. This time he went down with his back to it. If something was going to get him, he wanted to see it coming.

He made it across the kitchen and out to the porch in a couple of seconds. Standing at the edge of the porch with his long nightshirt flapping in the breeze from the bay, he heard Coon Dog gnawing on chicken bones over near the shed where he slept.

Thomas went down the porch steps. "Hey, CD. Hey, you old coon dog. Come on over here now," he whispered.

The old hound dog stopped gnawing for a minute

and said something in dog talk to Thomas.

"Come on with me now," Thomas whispered. "You can bring one of them bones with you."

Coon Dog got to his feet slowly and then stretched himself out again at Thomas's feet, whining as if he were happy for the nighttime visit.

Thomas caught him by the collar. "How'd you like to sleep in the loft with me, old boy? How would that be? Come on now. Let's get in 'fore somebody sees us."

Coon Dog started up on the porch willingly, but hesitated at the kitchen door. Thomas pulled at him. "Lucy ain't here now, old boy. Ain't nobody gonna run you off."

Coon Dog crouched low and whined, this time unhappily.

Thomas thought uneasily that Coon Dog must be afraid of something besides Lucy.

No matter, scared or not, the dog was going to have to come with him. He pulled him across the bare wooden floor and to the narrow steps of the ladder.

Coon Dog balked again at the ladder, clearly thinking Thomas was asking too much of him. Thomas pulled hard. "Come on now, boy. You can do it."

Coon Dog put his paws on the narrow rungs of the ladder and made an unwilling effort. His big paws slid awkwardly on the steps, and he tried to pull back. Thomas stubbornly held on to his collar and kept tugging him on.

They made it about halfway up when Coon Dog's back paws slipped through the steps. He did a flip backward, hit the top of a sideboard with a wild crash, and bounced off to the floor.

Righting himself, he ran for the kitchen door, but Thomas had closed it. Coon Dog stretched himself up on it, clawing away at Lucy's aprons and towels that hung there.

"Quit it, you fool dog," Thomas said, pushing him away from the door so he could open it. Coon Dog was out like a bolt of lightning, leaving Thomas peering into the dark kitchen at the wreckage Coon Dog had left behind.

Light fell across the kitchen floor, and Thomas wheeled around. There stood Aunt Lena, big as a mountain, holding a kerosene lamp high. Her mouth was caved in because she hadn't stopped to put in her teeth. Her black eyes blazed in the lamplight. Her hair was in a huge white nightcap, and she was clutching a crazy quilt around her.

"What in our dear Lord's name are you up to?" she demanded.

"I, uh, was just getting something to eat."

"Sherman's army didn't make this much mess getting something to eat."

There wasn't anything for him to say. If he told her what had happened, she'd be even angrier.

She tromped over to the sideboard to survey the damage. Flour and sugar were thick on top of the sideboard and on the floor in front of it. "Look! You've broken your mama's best stoneware cannisters. What will she say?"

Thomas hung his head. He felt miserable. What would she say indeed? More important, how would she feel?

"Trouble is your middle name, Thomas. You must take after your daddy, God rest his soul."

"I—I'll clean it up."

"No, you won't. You'll go on up to the loft and go to sleep. Lucy'll take care of it in the morning, and you, too, probably. But nothing can bring back your mama's pretty things. Go on to bed now. And don't you stir out of that loft until Lucy gets here."

She held the lamp high, watching him climb the ladder. He clambered over the ledge, then looked back at her. "I didn't mean to do it, Aunt Lena."

"Humph!" Her black eyes looked enormous in the shadows cast by the lamp. She nodded. "You probably didn't. I'll give you that. You probably didn't."

She went out, closing the kitchen door firmly behind her.

Thomas crept across the floor of the loft to the small trunk nestled under the eaves. He turned over the few pieces of clothing there, trying to decide what was the best thing to run away in.

It was the only thing to do. The Parker crowd had moved in on him, and his mother seemed to think more of Mr. Parker than she did of him. She'd think even less when she saw her stoneware all broken up. He's just as well go on and leave now while he had a good chance.

Tonight he'd go sleep in one of the boats tied under the pier. Early in the morning he'd go to his hideout in the mangrove thicket and figure out a way to get to Tampa—Cuba, maybe.

The gate creaked when he opened it about ten minutes later, but the house stayed dark and quiet. It looked different in the moonlight, its white paint glowing softly, as ghostlike as the kitchen had been. It didn't seem much like his house anymore.

A wet nose touched his hand. Coon Dog had followed him through the gate.

"You old Coon Dog, you. You think you're gonna go with me, don't you?" He thought a minute. "Well, you might as well. You're in right much trouble yourself."

SIX

THE MANGROVE HIDEOUT

Olivia Parker tugged at her husband's arm, urging him to hurry. They were almost home again, and she was anxious to see Thomas and find out how he'd behaved in her absence.

She felt sure she had done the right thing in marrying Mr. Parker, but she also felt a little guilty since Thomas had been so much against the idea.

She pushed the soft brown curls away from her face, her hazel eyes staring toward the small white house.

Suddenly the two little girls burst through the door, followed by Lucy. Thomas was not to be seen. Olivia began to feel uneasy. She had really hoped he'd meet them at the dock when the steamer came in.

The girls flung themselves in their father's arms. "We want to tell you something," Pearl burst out, "but we dasn't. Lucy says she wants to be the first to tell you."

Olivia caught Lucy's arm. "What is it? Where's Thomas? Has something happened to Thomas?"

"No, ma'am. Rest easy now. He's just up to some of his old tricks. Y'all come in the house now and get a cool drink of water. I just drew some from the well."

Olivia started for the porch, fanning herself with her wide-brimmed hat. Once there she turned to Lucy. "Where is he?" she demanded. "Tell me this instant!"

"Well, Thomas just done run off again. He left sometime in the night after the wedding. There wasn't no way we could let you know. Besides, Coon Dog has trotted in and out of here natural as you please, so we figure Thomas is all right. He got food from the preacher's kitchen both nights."

"The little scamp," Mr. Parker said.

Olivia gave him a hurt look, and he added, "Just a manner of speaking, dear." He cleared his throat. "You say he's run off again. Do you mean he makes this a habit?"

"It's just a little-boy kind of thing he does," Olivia explained. "When he gets in trouble or doesn't want to do something he's told to do, he goes off somewhere. He used to hide in the hall closet, but then he started going to Hal's or to some neighbor's barn. He's never stayed this long."

Olivia looked at the two girls, who were listening with self-righteous expressions on their faces. "All children have childish tricks they try from time to time."

Their smiles faded.

Mr. Parker said, "Did you young ones have anything to do with Thomas running away?"

"Oh, no, Papa."

Lucy spoke up. "I 'spect Hal knows where he is, but he ain't telling."

Olivia nodded in agreement. "Lucy, you go get Hal, and Brother Watson if he can come. I'm going to change into a day dress. I'll be ready by the time you get back."

Mr. Parker spoke up. "I'll stay with you until the preacher comes, and then I must go to the store. Lord knows what has happened to my business while I've been gone."

"Well, you don't have to wait, dear," Olivia said. "I can handle this." She looked over at the girls standing quietly at the side of the porch and touched his arm. "Why don't you take our bags upstairs and then go on to the store? I'll get out the surprises we brought for the children."

Pearl and Indigo jumped up and down, their mouths round *o*'s of excitement.

Mr. Parker picked up the bags. "Mrs. Parker, dear, I plan to stay here until we find out more about this matter. I'm head of this household now, and I'd like to take care of this situation in my own way."

He went into the house with his daughters dancing behind him, and Olivia and Lucy stared at each other unhappily, wondering what his way might be.

Hal wasn't particularly afraid walking over to Thomas's house with his father. He truly didn't know where

Thomas was, so he didn't have to lie or snitch either.

When Lucy showed them into the parlor, he began to feel afraid. Nobody sat in a parlor unless somebody was dead or the bishop was coming to visit.

Thomas's mother jumped up as soon as she saw him. "Where's Thomas, Hal? I'm sure you know."

Hal shook his head. "But I don't, ma'am. I already looked in all the places I could think of he might be hiding."

"But didn't you give him food from your kitchen?"

Hal shook his head and looked at his father helplessly. It was his father who had told Lucy about the missing food. Why didn't he speak up now?

Just then he did. "There were signs of a raider at our house," his father said with a half smile. "I only guessed it was Thomas since he's rather familiar with our kitchen. I told Lucy to ease her mind some."

Mr. Parker stared hard at Hal. "But you really hadn't seen him at your house or anywhere else while we were gone?" Before Hal could even answer, Mr. Parker shook his head. "I find that just a little hard to believe."

Hal's father nodded. "I find it hard to believe myself, and if you're not telling the truth, son, Judgment Day is coming, and I don't mean in glory either."

"But I *am* telling the truth," Hal said.

Mr. Parker sighed. "Well, Brother Watson, perhaps you should close and latch your shutters tonight so the little rascal can't get in and eat."

Thomas's mother had been fidgeting in her chair. Now she jumped up. "Mr. Parker, I do protest."

"I'm sorry, my dear. I don't mean to sound unduly harsh, but if the boy gets really hungry, he's certainly more likely to come home. That's what we want, isn't it?"

She looked at him uncertainly, but she didn't say anymore. After a moment Hal and his father left—for which Hal was very grateful.

Thomas woke up from his nap under the mangrove trees, feeling hot and hungry. He sat up and pulled his stockings down to scratch at the dark red bites around his ankles and under his kneecaps. Plagued chiggers!

He wondered what time it was. His stomach felt so empty he figured it must be getting pretty late in the day. He pushed aside the thick mangrove branches to see how low the sun had fallen over the bay.

It was dropping mighty slowly. Hot and bright, its light glistened on the rippling water. He sighed in disappointment. It would be a couple of hours before the sun sank below the water, coloring the water and the massed clouds above it with pinks and purples.

He didn't care a hoot about the sunset. He wanted it to happen in a hurry so he could go scavenging for food. And for water. He was perishing for a drink of cold water. The Mason jar he'd gotten out of the preacher's kitchen was bone dry.

He crawled a little further into the shade of a twisted mangrove tree and stretched out to sleep again. That was about all he could do right now. Sleep or think.

He had to make a decision soon. He either had to go

on and really run far away, or he had to go back home. He couldn't stay hidden here in town forever.

There were a couple of ways he could leave. He could follow the dirt road through the woods and swamps to Tampa. The trouble with that was he might get off on a side trail and get lost. Since he didn't have his gun to shoot squirrels or any kind of rig for fishing, he might starve. Besides that, he could run into renegade Indians he'd heard tales about, or cattle rustlers. He didn't know which was worse.

He could be a stowaway on a boat to Tampa. The trick would be to hide around the pier while the boat was being loaded and later sneak aboard without being seen. By then everybody in town would know he had run away. They'd tell his mother the minute he was spotted, or worse, they'd drag him home by the hair of his head. He wouldn't mind being dragged home, really, if it was only to his mother. But now there were Mr. Parker and the girls.

The girls! That Indigo had probably already been under the house working away to find the treasure. He couldn't run off now and leave all that to her!

Thomas groaned. He couldn't win for losing. He wasn't sure if even finding the treasure was worth having to live with Mr. Parker and those girls.

He lay back down again and curled up on his side. He felt miserable in body and mind. Maybe he was coming down with the yellow fever. This thought pleased him a little. He could even die. Then they'd feel sorry for all the mean things they had done to him!

Thomas lay with his face toward the water. The slick mud, washed over by small waves, was pockmarked with fiddler crab holes. When he lay very still, the tiny gray-brown crabs came out of their holes, scouting for food. If he so much as moved an eyelash, they would slide back into their holes in precision form, as if some commander had given them a signal.

So, there they were, safe in their little hidey holes, and here he was, tired and hot and hungry and thirsty and maybe dying of the yellow fever!

Suddenly, Thomas thought of where he could at least spend the night. As soon as it got good and dark, he would go back to the preacher's kitchen for more food. Then he would go over and sleep in the church. The Bible said the sanctuary was a place to hide from your enemies. They couldn't beat on you or kill you when you were in the sanctuary.

Tonight Thomas was feeling like he had a lot of enemies.

When it was almost dark, Thomas began to make his way through the shallow water at the edge of the bay toward the pier at the foot of Main Street. He wanted to see if a steamer had come in today to load on citrus or fish.

Folks living in the half dozen houses built along the bay would be inside eating supper or out back doing chores. The guests who might be sitting on the piazza at the hotel next to the pier wouldn't know him. He had only to avoid fishermen who might be making their way in from the gulf or one of the islands offshore.

There wasn't a steamer at the pier, only a few rowboats tied up near the shore. In the seafood restaurant built on the pier, people were eating and talking and laughing. It made Thomas feel very lonely. He clung close to a barnacle-covered piling, letting the water wash over his mosquito-chewed ankles, and waited for dark.

When he was sure it was quite safe, Thomas headed up Main Street toward Five Points. The first thing he wanted to do was get a long drink of water from the well there. He stepped nimbly around the cows that were settling down in the sandy street for the night. The new kerosene street lamp hanging over the well and the watering trough around it cast shadows behind him as he ran. Thomas wasn't too worried. Nobody was in sight, and if anyone appeared, he could get his drink and get away in plenty of time.

The church was just across the way. In the daytime, with people moving in and out, it looked a lot friendlier than it did tonight. He hesitated a moment and stared at the belfry, which, lifted up against the night sky, topped the roofs of the livery stable and the markets on the other corners of Five Points.

He quickly got his drink and headed for Hal's house. Maybe hiding in the dark little church wasn't such a good idea after all. The steeple pointing toward heaven had reminded Thomas of God. And God couldn't be too happy with him right now.

When Thomas came under Hal's window, he was tempted to throw something up there and wake him up. He had missed his friend terribly the last couple of days. Instead, Thomas shook his head and moved alongside the long, narrow house. He might just wake up the preacher, after all.

A rotting stump of a tree just under the kitchen window was just right to stand on and to help pull himself through the window and into the kitchen. Resting a moment on the windowsill, he stared into the dark room. He could see the outline of the cookstove right in the middle, taking up most of the floor space.

Thomas hoped there would be some leftovers in the warming oven at the top of the stove—bread, or even a leg of fried rabbit. Last night he'd found beans on the stove and a plate and fork on the table laid out as if somebody had known he was coming. Probably good old Hal.

Thomas moved toward the stove and then froze in his tracks. Someone else was in the kitchen—a dark form standing on the other side of the stove.

Hal? No, not Hal. Too big for Hal.

He wheeled to run, but the form moved faster. Before Thomas could scramble out the window, his arms were pinned to his sides and he was trapped against somebody big and strong.

Thomas's heart beat fast. Who had him? A rustler? An Indian? Mr. Parker?

"Rest yourself easy," a voice said quietly. It was the preacher.

Thomas felt only slightly relieved. "I—I was just getting something to eat. I—I'll pay it back. I'll even bring extra."

▲54

The preacher released him, and Thomas moved to escape. He was caught again by one arm. "You can't get something to eat if you don't stay a few minutes. Here, come sit at the table. I've laid some supper out for you."

Thomas felt himself being pulled across the kitchen floor, and in a moment the preacher shoved him firmly into a chair.

Sure enough, the table was set with a plate of food and a tall glass of milk. There was even a piece of chocolate cake sitting beside a huge linen napkin.

Thomas stared at the feast. He had no plans to run away at this moment.

The preacher moved over to the counter, struck a flint, and lighted a kerosene lamp.

Thomas spoke up in alarm. "Somebody will see me!"

The preacher sat down at the table across from him. "I doubt it. Who's roaming around this time of evening, except you and me? And God, of course."

Thomas groaned. "He probably is angry as all get out with me."

"Well, he certainly isn't pleased with you. You've worried your mother and upset your new family. Of course, you can change all that in a hurry. You can start by just being sorry for what you've done. Tell the Lord you're sorry. Then apologize to your parents. And of course, you should make up your mind right now never to pull a stunt like this again."

Thomas had been keeping one eye on his plate and another on the preacher. He'd been nodding his head through the sorry part, and even the apology part. But when the preacher got to the promise never to run away again, he stopped nodding.

"I can see you're having a hard time with my suggestions. I believe I need to lift you up in prayer," the preacher said.

"Right now?" Thomas cried. He had a vision of Brother Watson on his knees, praying out loud for the Lord and everybody else in town to hear. He moved quickly to touch the preacher's arm. "That's all right, Brother Watson. I wouldn't bother the Lord right now. It's pretty late at night."

The preacher smiled. "I expect the Lord stays up late just in case there's someone like you who needs to repent."

Thomas nodded. "Yes, sir, I 'spect he does that. And I'll work on the repenting. I promise."

The preacher got up from the table. "I'm going to hold you to that promise, my young friend. But right now I'll go along to bed so you can eat in peace. I've laid out for you a pallet of quilts over by the door. I'm trusting you to finish your supper and sleep here tonight. I've already told my wife you'll be here. She'll give you an early breakfast and fix a tub of water for you to bathe. You wouldn't want to go home as dirty as you are."

Thomas felt a funny kind of hope stirring. "You're going to make me go home, aren't you?"

The preacher smiled. "Let's say I'm going to encourage you, should you falter."

PUNISHMENT IN THE PARLOR

Thomas timed himself to get home around eight o'clock. He figured Mr. Parker would have gone to the grocery store long before then. And if he was really lucky, the girls would be off playing with some of their silly friends. He came in through the front gate and was walking down the wide center hall of the house before he realized he had guessed wrong.

Mr. Parker came out of the sitting room behind the parlor to meet him. He was dressed to go to work all right. Black pants and suspenders, white shirt, high collar, and long black tie all put together in perfect neatness. All the men who worked in the stores and offices wore the same outfits, but on Mr. Parker it somehow looked different, strict, like the school-marm's yardstick.

Thomas's mother came running behind. She pushed

past Mr. Parker to catch Thomas in her arms. "Thomas, baby, where have you been?"

Thomas allowed himself to be hugged. Under the circumstances it seemed like a good idea.

"Where did you go?" she asked anxiously. "Where did you sleep? Look at you—all mosquito bites and scratches!"

Mr. Parker stepped over and separated the two of them with his long, strong hands. He didn't look angry, but he was certainly serious. "Come into the sitting room now," he said. He stood at one side of the door, beckoning them to go in. Inside he nodded that his wife should sit on the small divan. Thomas moved quickly to sit by her, but Mr. Parker caught his arm and waved him toward a single wooden chair well away from the divan. He himself then sat down in another chair facing Thomas.

Thomas heard a muffled giggle and noticed for the first time that Indigo and Pearl were in the room, too, sitting at the round table in the corner. Mr. Parker frowned at them, and they became silent. He took his gold watch out of his pocket and studied it. Then he looked at Thomas over it. "You've made me late at the store, very late. I wanted, however, to be here when you came."

"How—how did you know I was coming?" Thomas stuttered.

"Brother Watson stopped by here early," his mother said. "We were so relieved to know you were safe, dear. We've been so terribly worried."

Mr. Parker frowned at his watch and put it back in

his pocket. "I'll stay one minute more. Tonight we'll have a real talk, Thomas. Just the two of us. Now, answer your mother's questions. Where have you been? Where did you stay at night?"

Thomas moved uneasily in his chair. He wasn't going to tell about his hiding place in the mangrove thicket. He might need to go there again, most anytime, in fact. "Well, I moved around a lot. I stayed in the woods during the day mostly. One night I slept in a boat under the pier. The mosquitoes were fierce. The next night I slept in a shed by the fish house." He made a face. "The rats ran over me there."

His mother was fanning herself with her handkerchief and making little worried sounds. "Oh, my dear. Oh, my dear. How dreadful. I just hoped Hal had hidden you in his room and you were safe."

"I didn't want to stay there and maybe get him in trouble," Thomas said. That wasn't exactly true, but it seemed to be a pretty good thing to say. He hadn't been able to get near Hal during the day, and at night he was afraid of trying to get up in his room for fear of waking the rest of the family.

Mr. Parker got up. "I've got to get to the store now. No telling what that lazy Wiley boy has done or failed to do by now." He turned to his wife. "Olivia, my dear, I think Thomas should go to the parlor and sit the rest of the day. After supper tonight he and I can have a good talk about some of the things I've already discussed with you. Don't you agree, my dear?"

For one moment his mother looked at him like his own private mother again. Her hazel eyes flashed, her chin firmed up. She looked as if she might say, "I don't agree at all. I think Thomas should go to the kitchen for something good to eat and then go out and play." But she didn't say anything. The spark in her eyes faded, and she sighed. Then she said, "I think you're probably right, Mr. Parker, dear." She looked away from Thomas.

Inside, Thomas felt as if someone had pressed him flat with a millstone. He sat perfectly still as she got up and started out of the room after her husband.

As she passed Thomas, she reached out to put her hand on his shoulder. "It's all going to work out for the best, Thomas." She gave his shoulder a soft little squeeze and left.

He doubted her words, but the pain in his chest eased up a little. She still loved him some, anyhow.

The girls snickered as they simpered toward him on the way out of the room. Pearl made sure both adults were well out of sight and then stuck her tongue out at him.

She started to run, and Thomas, without a thought, stuck out his foot and tripped her. Pearl went sprawling on the floor, skirts and petticoats flying, high-booted feet flailing like march reeds in the wind.

"Run-runhhhhh," she wailed.

Mr. Parker came running back in a hurry. "What happened, what happened?"

Indigo was pulling Pearl up roughly and shaking her to her feet like a large rag doll. "Nothing," Indigo said. "She just stumbled and fell. She's all right now, aren't you, Pearl?" She fixed Pearl with a glare. Pearl shook her perspiring head that yes, she was all right.

"We'll go along now, Father," Indigo said. "We'll get right at our chores. Come on, Pearl. When we're finished, I'll give you a peppermint."

Thomas had sat in the parlor an hour. Unfortunately he had chosen a wooden chair by the window. His tailbone was numb, and no amount of moving about eased the pain. He wasn't sure if Mr. Parker meant he was to sit in the same chair or just in the parlor. With those two spying girls around, he'd decided to stay in one place, at least until noon when the family ate dinner.

Nobody had suggested he couldn't eat dinner. And nobody, under any circumstances, ever ate in the parlor. He was bound to get a break then.

He shifted again, resting his elbow on the arm of the chair and his face in his hand. If he had some way to lean his head back, he might go to sleep. Quiet steps in the hall caught his attention. Maybe his mother had come to rescue him at last.

In a moment Indigo moved silently into the room, her thin face unsmiling but somehow excited.

"Get out of here," he growled. "I don't want to talk to no girls."

She came in anyway and planted herself in front of him. "Did you really hide in the woods and sleep in the shack with the rats?"

"Of course, silly, what do you think I did?"

"I still think you could have slept with Hal."

"You ought to know I couldn't get in to Hal. He

sleeps upstairs next to his pa. I never knew when his pa might be awake thinking about sinners or praying or something like that. Besides 'he never slumbers or sleeps.'" That expression had come to his mind from somewhere.

"That Bible verse is talking about God," Indigo said scornfully.

"Humph. I know that. But it fits the preacher, too."

She thought for a minute and then nodded. "Well, if you really did hide out like that, you're brave. But I think you must have been scared, too, some of the time."

Thomas shrugged his shoulders. "Naaa, I wasn't scared." That was a lie. He'd been scared, at least part of the time, both nights.

She took a step closer to him. "How about when you dug for the treasure? Was that scary?"

Thomas almost came up out of his chair. "Have you been under this house?"

She put her hands on her hips and pursed her lips. "Of course not. My father wouldn't allow it. He would say it was unladylike." She cocked her head to one side and raised her eyebrows. "Of course, if he would allow it—and you would allow it—I'd be under there in a minute."

"I wouldn't allow it."

Thomas studied Indigo. Her nearly black hair was in tight pigtails hanging behind big ears. Her thin lips were very red, and her black eyes glinted like shiny buttons. She was wearing a plain dark skirt with a white blouse and a silly little string tie down the front. She looked pretty ugly, even for a girl.

But she wasn't as dumb as he'd thought. He shrugged again. "Sometimes I get scared. Different things scare me. Just a little bit."

She nodded. Smoothing her square hands down her skirt, she said, "If you ever decide to run away again, will you let me go with you?"

Thomas fell back in his chair in horror. "Me? Run away with a girl?"

Indigo dropped her head and turned as if she were going to run from the room.

"Why would you want to leave anyhow?" Thomas demanded. "You and your pa moved in here and took over everything. You even got my bedroom!"

She shook her head furiously. "No, I haven't. I'm just sleeping in your dumb old room. My room is back in Massachusetts!"

This time she did run out of the room.

EIGHT

A NEW JOB

As soon as supper was over that evening, Mr. Parker told Thomas the two of them were going for a walk.

Walk was all Mr. Parker seemed to want to do. They went down the sandy road toward town with no conversation. If they passed somebody out for a stroll, Mr. Parker would say, "Howdy," or "Evening," or maybe, " 'Sa pleasant evening." If it was a lady, he tipped his hat.

Thomas didn't say anything. He was embarrassed to be out walking with Mr. Parker and hoped they didn't run into any of his friends.

When they got to Five Points, they walked down the wooden sidewalk to the pier. The last of the sunset shone in a pink glow behind heavy dark clouds. They didn't go out on the pier to check the water or the tide or the fish or anything interesting like that. They just turned around and started back up Main Street on the other side until they came to Mr. Parker's store on the corner.

Thomas didn't even want to look at the store. He felt it was the store's fault that his mother and Mr. Parker had gotten together in the first place.

Mr. Parker unlocked the door and went in. Thomas followed unhappily. In spite of himself his eyes went to the candy counter. Even in the shadows he could see the peppermint sticks, lemon drops, and taffy chews. Thomas's mouth watered, but Mr. Parker didn't offer him any candy.

He must have noticed Thomas looking at it. "You won't be allowed to help yourself to candy now, anymore than before, Thomas. My girls aren't allowed either. Can't have you eating up the profits, you know."

Thomas nodded. *Stingy*, he thought to himself. He didn't care. His mother would give him pennies to buy candy when he wanted it. And he would buy it from Turner's Store, not this one.

Mr. Parker didn't light the lamp, but leaned against the counter by the polished brass cash register. Thomas didn't know what he was supposed to do, so he took a seat on a short board stretched over a small barrel.

Mr. Parker continued to study him, and Thomas felt more unhappy by the moment. At last Mr. Parker spoke up.

"Thomas, we're off to a terrible start. Obviously, you don't like me, and you've made it hard for me to like you."

Thomas was shocked. Grown-ups had never suggested to him that they didn't like him. Not right up to his face. They might say, "You're a wicked boy," or "I wash my hands of you," or even "God's going to punish you." But not a flat-out "I don't like you." Hearing it gave Thomas an empty feeling he hadn't felt before.

He kept still but he could think, and think he did. If Mr. Parker had told his mother he didn't like him, she wouldn't have married him. Thomas was sure of that.

Mr. Parker was watching him closely as if he could read his mind. Thomas tightened his jaw, hoping that would affect his brain, too.

Mr. Parker said, "I think it's best to speak plainly, and so I have and will. I think you've had too many women around you since your father and grandfather died. They've spoiled you and kept you a baby. It's time you grew up. I would like to help you do that."

Thomas didn't know how that could be done, but it didn't sound pleasant.

"I think the best way to start is for you to begin working in the afternoons until school is out. Then you can work all day. I was working in a dry goods store for my father before I was ten."

"But where would I work?" Thomas was remembering what Indigo had said earlier and was afraid it was true.

"Here at my store. I've talked to your mother and she agrees it would be a good idea. You can deliver groceries and help me keep the place clean. I'm going to let Wiley go, and train you to take his place."

Thomas felt a small amount of interest stir. Delivering groceries or maybe heavy supplies in a wagon could be fun. "Could I drive a horse and wagon?"

"Well, not right away. You're not trained to handle a horse. When you're older and have shown me you're responsible, I may get Hooper to teach you."

Thomas's hopes for something exciting by way of a job faded. Hooper was Lucy's husband. He was old as Christmas and would probably be dead before Mr. Parker figured Thomas was ready to drive a wagon.

"But how would I carry the groceries?" Thomas asked.

"In your arms, you lazy boy," Mr. Parker replied. "Or in your own wagon. I saw it out in the shed yesterday. Looks like you've never used it."

Thomas dropped his head and rubbed his bare toes on the worn wood of the floor. "My father built it for me. He was going to get me a goat to pull it, but he died."

Mr. Parker cleared his throat. "Yes, I'm sorry about that. But of course, I can't buy you a goat right now. And to be honest with you, after some of the things I've heard, I'd worry you might get in the wagon and take off somewhere."

Thomas rubbed his toes on the floor some more.

"Actually the wagon is not too big for you to pull yourself. I want you to get it out and clean it first chance you get. But tomorrow morning I want you to come on with me to the store."

Thomas could hardly believe this was happening. He hedged for time. "Saturday morning? But me and Hal's planning to catch the first tide and go fishing!" What he was really planning was to get hold of Hal and start some serious digging, but he had a clear notion Mr. Parker wouldn't take to that idea at all.

Mr. Parker shook his head. "That's not really true, is it? You and Hal haven't seen each other to plan a fishing trip."

Thomas protested. "Well, it's true in a way. Hal and me said we were going fishing first chance we got after the wedding. This is the first chance, so I wasn't telling a story, was I?"

"Well, you were certainly stretching the truth. It's not a good habit, Thomas." He moved away from the counter, went to stare out the door for a moment, and then came back. "I think you ought to stop calling me Mr. Parker. Doesn't seem right. What did you call your real father?"

"I don't know." This was a real lie. "I was awful little when he died." He looked away. His mother had told him over and over the name he'd called his father. Whenever he heard his father's horse on the path, he'd run to the door crying, "Papapa, Papapa!"

"Well, I'm sure it would seem unnatural for you to say, 'Papa,' as my girls do. Perhaps you can just say, 'Pa.'"

Thomas gulped. "I'll try, Mr. Parker." And that was another lie. He planned to avoid having to call him anything at all.

Mr. Parker started walking toward the door again. "Let's get back to the house. I want us all to start getting up earlier. It's the early bird that catches the worm, you know."

Thomas groaned inside himself, but started trudging down the road after his stepfather. The only reason to catch worms was to go fishing, and Mr. Parker didn't understand that at all!

They were almost at the house when Mr. Parker stopped walking. He faced Thomas and said, "Just because we started out badly doesn't mean it has to stay that way. I'm willing to try for a fresh start if you'll meet me halfway."

Thomas looked desperately toward the house, hoping for some interruption to save him from having to answer Mr. Parker. For once the girls did something right. They came charging out of the house and out the gate like puppies escaping a pen.

"We're going to play Dominoes with Thomas," they cried, as if Thomas weren't even standing there. "His mother said so. We're going to be just like a real family!"

Thomas walked quickly on ahead of them. They weren't a real family, and his mother couldn't make them one just by saying the words.

When he got to the house, he would have made a break for the loft, but she was standing at the foot of the steps. She caught his arm and walked him into the house. In the sitting room he saw she'd lit a lamp for the round table and set out the dominoes.

She gave his arm a little tug. "Just one game, honey," she coaxed. "Help Indigo teach Pearl how to play."

It was important to his mother for him to agree. He knew that. Not wanting to embarrass her in front of the others, he sank down in a chair at the table and turned toward Indigo.

69

"Well, come on then," he said with a scowl. "I'll show you how it's done."

Thomas didn't have to show Indigo anything. She was very good at Dominoes. Her eyes sparkled in the lamplight as she studied the black bones in front of her. Her fingers moved quickly, matching the right piece to the set time after time. Even though she was coaching Pearl as she played, she managed to win the game.

Disgusted, Thomas quickly began turning the bones face-down for another try. She wasn't going to beat him again. He hardly noticed when Pearl slid out of her chair, saying she was sleepy. Thomas concentrated on the game, forgetting how much he disliked Indigo.

In a little while he put his final bone in place and sat back grinning.

"You're pretty good," Indigo said. "Two out of three?"

Mr. Parker sat down in the chair Pearl had left. "How about playing me a game, Thomas? I used to be pretty good at this myself."

Thomas stared at him. For just one second he really wanted to take him on. But then he remembered who Mr. Parker was and what he had done to ruin his life. He pushed back his chair. "Well, no, thanks," he said. "I'm pretty tired. And like you said, we got to get up in the morning and catch worms."

Mr. Parker looked down at the table and then began to stack the dominoes neatly back in the long, narrow box.

"Well, good night all," Thomas said, wanting to get out of the room in a hurry. The sight of Mr. Parker silently putting away the dominoes was making him feel bad.

Indigo got up, too. "Good night, Thomas. Don't let the haunt get you."

Thomas blinked. He hadn't had time to think about the haunt the last couple of hours. He had thought about it when he was alone in the parlor and had even considered asking his mother to let him sleep in here on the divan. But now, with them all looking at him and Indigo grinning, he was blamed if he'd say anything.

"Haunt, indeed," his mother said, coming over to kiss his cheek. She looked unhappy with him. Thomas didn't think it was about the haunt in the loft. He thought it was about Mr. Parker and the Dominoes game.

Lying on his pallet in the loft, he tried to get rid of his own unhappy feelings. *It's not my fault,* he thought. *It's his fault. He moved in on me and Mama and ordered me to start working in his old store. He said he didn't even like me!*

Thomas thought some more, gradually feeling sleep come on. *Does he think now all he has to do is play a game of Dominoes and we're friends?* he half-muttered to himself.

Thomas punched his big feather pillow into a new shape and tried to relax against it. He heard sounds of the family moving about the main house getting ready for bed. Someone came out on the porch and worked the pump to get water. Then the door closed, and everything was quiet from that quarter.

Staring at the small triangle of space under the eaves, he listened to the night sounds outside—the wind soughing through the trees, an occasional pop on the roof when something fell against the tin, a bird in the oak near the cookhouse talking to itself.

Thomas identified each sound to his own satisfaction. He hadn't needed Indigo's taunt to remind him of the cookhouse ghost.

And then he heard it—a sound different from all the rest—a brisk little buzzing sound, a tiny clacking like the smallest of bones shaken together in a box. A buzzing rattling, close by.

Thomas's eyes flew wide open. What he was hearing was the warning of a rattlesnake startled on the path, daring a body to come closer.

Thomas began to perspire, remembering the old sailor digging under the house, struck from out of nowhere by a rattler. But how could a rattlesnake get into the loft? He couldn't. Coon Dog must have stirred one up in the yard.

The tiny vibrating sound came again. It was closer than the yard, if not in the loft, then in the kitchen for sure.

Thomas listened, wide-eyed, trying not to move a muscle. He heard a soft creak of the boards in the kitchen below. There was no other sound. Not a door opening and shutting. Not anything.

After a while he began to relax, and his eyes grew heavy. It couldn't have been a rattler. Not in the night. It was Hal trying to scare him. Hal knew about Lucy's tall tales. Thomas closed his eyes and willed himself to go to sleep. In the morning he'd get that Hal.

Early the next morning Mr. Parker woke him up to go to work. At the breakfast table Mr. Parker said, "I'm going on ahead. I have some bookwork to do before you come. But don't be too long now."

"I won't," Thomas said unhappily. Last night he had forgotten all about going to work. The rattlesnake had scared the idea right out of him.

He didn't say anything about the snake's warning. He figured the family would just say he was dreaming or some such dumb thing. But he intended to see Hal.

"I have to go by the preacher's," he told Mr. Parker. "I have to tell Hal why I can't go fishing."

"Well, that's the courteous thing to do," Mr. Parker said. "But don't dillydally."

"I won't," Thomas said. He'd stay just long enough to put a lump on Hal's head, but he didn't dare tell that to Mr. Parker. When he got to the preacher's, he asked for his friend, then he poured out the events of the evening before.

Hal listened with interest to Thomas's tale, even through the accusation part. Finally he protested. "But I couldn't have done it! I would have if I'd thought of it, but I didn't. Besides, I couldn't. I was over to Fruitville with Pa last night. We were there at the Busbee's house nearly till dawn. Old man Busbee's trying to kick the bucket."

"It was long before dawn, I know," Thomas said slowly, still suspicious.

"Then it couldn't a been me. Ask Pa." He stopped a minute. "I bet it was those girls."

Thomas shook his head in disgust. "Hal, you know better! Girls don't fool with rattlesnakes." He stopped, a new thought in his mind. Hal wouldn't play with a live rattler either. And neither would Sample. Sample devoted himself to killing them.

Then who and why?

"You probably just imagined the sound," Hal said. "It's easy to imagine a sound like that when you're alone in the dark."

"I didn't imagine it!" Thomas cried indignantly.

They both grew quiet. After a moment Hal said, "Do you think rattlesnakes have ghosts?"

Thomas nodded grimly. He'd already come to that very conclusion. "You see what this means?" he said, leaning near Hal and almost whispering.

"It means I'm not going near your cookhouse," Hal said.

Thomas gave him a shove, then grabbed him by the shirt and pulled him back up close. "It means I'm making the ghost very nervous."

"Well, that's two of us you're making very nervous," Hal said, pulling away.

"Dummy! Don't you see it means we're close to his plagued old coins! All we got to do is go get 'em."

74

NINE

WIND OR
WEIRDNESS?

Thomas saw immediately it wasn't going to be easy to find time to hunt the treasure. He had to get up early to go to school and then go right to the store to work. When he got home from work, it was past five o'clock and nearly supper time. After supper he had to do his homework before he could go out to play.

To play! It was hard for Thomas to remember that just a short time back he had had all the time to play he wanted.

Up to now Mr. Parker didn't know anything about the ghost or the treasure. It was as if all the others in the family knew what he'd say if they told him and feared they'd be the one he'd jump on for talking such nonsense.

Thomas kept his digging time limited to those few minutes when Mr. Parker still hadn't come home or those evenings when he went back to work. Sometimes Mr. Parker reappeared while Thomas was still working under the house. Then Thomas would keep still and follow Mr. Parker's footsteps into the house so he could crawl out the opposite end and run to the shed with the shovel.

Under these circumstances it was hard for Hal to know when to come to help, and Hal had his own homework to do.

One night at the supper table, Mr. Parker said, "I have to go to a conference meeting at the church tonight. Unfortunately, a matter of controversial nature is to be discussed, so I'm afraid I'll be late."

Thomas almost jumped off the bench, but caught himself in time and glued his eyes to his plate. He hoped and then prayed fiercely that Mr. Parker wouldn't give him some extra chore to take up this precious piece of time.

Indigo gave him a kick under the table. Without moving his eyes, he managed to return the kick, with good measure.

As soon as Mr. Parker excused himself and left the room, Thomas was off his place on the bench and next to his mother's chair. "Can I run get Hal?"

"May, Thomas," she corrected, knowing exactly what he had in mind. "What about your homework?"

Thomas fidgeted. "After my homework. I've just got a little." That wasn't true, but he'd do enough to keep his teacher from killing him tomorrow, and it was worth a halfway killing just to have this time to really dig.

Indigo knew he had a lot of homework because she

was in his group at school. He eyed her warily, but she didn't say anything.

As soon as the girls cleared away the dishes, he threw his books on the table and started working on what he considered the most crucial assignment. "I will pay attention in class. I will pay attention in class. I will pay attention in class. . . ."

By the time his mother had settled in her rocker, he had written it fifty times—half the assignment. He began closing his workbook, watching Indigo out of the corner of his eye. She pursed up her mouth, but kept working on the essay he also ought to be writing tonight.

He slammed the workbook shut. "Done!" he said, and before his mother could hardly look up from her sewing, he was out of the house.

Since Hal's father and mother were also at the conference, it wasn't hard to separate Hal from his chewed-up pencil and his homework.

Hal brought a shovel from his barn with him, and Thomas got his from the shed. They ran to the house, then dropped to their knees and began crawling under.

A moment later, Hal took Thomas's arm. "Now wait a minute, will you? We got to make some kind of plan."

"That's right," Thomas agreed reluctantly, hating to waste any time at all.

"We ought to start at one corner of the house and dig our way across, a little at a time."

"That'll take forever."

"It's going to take forever anyhow, and this way we won't dig in the same places over and over. I say we start at the front of the house and work back."

"It's not at the front of the house."

"How do you know?"

"Because the ghost haunts the cookhouse, and that's way to the back."

"Maybe that's just to trick you."

Thomas was doubtful. "Maybe." He thought a minute. "Let's just start at the back and work forward. We'd still be on a plan and near where the ghost is, too."

"All right, if you say so, but right now I'm going to take a stick and mark off squares under the whole house. Then we can work a square at a time."

Thomas had to admit Hal's plan made sense. "Go ahead and draw. I'm going to start digging in the first square as soon as you make it."

Thomas sat still a minute waiting for Hal to find a stick and start drawing. He eyed the heavy beams over their heads. They wouldn't have a lot of room to work in, and the long-handled shovels would make it even more difficult. They'd need short-handled spades, or maybe he'd just accidentally break off the handle of this shovel. . . .

It was beginning to get a little darker. Thomas eyed the shadows cast by the foundation pillars and the low tree stump cut when the house was built. They'd have to hurry. He didn't know when they'd get this much time again. And, there was another thing. At dark the haunt might just join them. Thomas grinned to himself. In the good daylight they still had, he didn't feel scared of the ghost at all.

"All right now," Hal said. "There's your first line of squares. Pick one end and start digging. I'll line up a couple more rows and start digging myself. I wouldn't mind being the one to turn up that gold."

"You won't," Thomas said matter-of-factly, then grabbed his shovel. He began working by the pillar at the most distant part of the house—back near the cookhouse.

They worked until the approaching night began making it harder for them to see. They didn't talk much, except to fuss when one of them threw a shovelful of sand too close to the other.

They had nothing to show for their effort. Nothing except piles of soft gray sand, bits of shell, a piece or two of an old kitchen plate and a few rusty nails.

By now they had worked up a full sweat that stung their eyes. When Thomas reached an arm up to dry off his forehead, the dirt smeared itself in wide paths across his face. His friend's face looked sooty, too.

Mosquitoes dogged them, and gnats got in their hair and stung like mischief across their scalps.

They had an idea what time it was. They had heard Lucy come tromping across the porch on her way home a good while back. She'd stopped long enough to holler at them, "Y'all better come out of there now. It's going to be dark in a shake. You got no business under there in the dark. You hear me, Thomas?"

"I hear you, I hear you. Go on home, you old worry wart."

She mumbled and grumbled and predicted all kinds of troubles in their direction, but after a while she left.

Sometimes the girls ran up and down the porch, stomping their feet. Once Indigo lay down and called over the edge of the porch, "Any luck?"

"Go finish your homework," Thomas said.

"I finished, which is a heap more than either of you did."

At that time Thomas's mother came and took the girls to bed, to Thomas's relief.

She let the boys continue to work until it was really too dark under the house for them to see much. Then she called to Thomas, "Come out right now, son. And I mean right now, before Mr. Parker comes home!"

Thomas and Hal looked at each other. *She's right,* Thomas thought, then asked his friend, "What about if we both go on out and get ourselves to bed like usual? And when all the grown people are settled in for the night, we can come right back, with a kerosene lamp."

"You're crazy, Thomas!"

"No, I'm not. We're never going to cover all this space under here at the rate we're going now."

Hal picked up his shovel. "Mr. Parker wouldn't like your plan at all. I mean, he just wouldn't like it at all."

"He'll never know. He'll be up there in the bedroom snoring, and we'll be way way off down here under the cookhouse."

The minute he said it, Thomas thought of somebody else who wouldn't like it—the ghost. Hal must have thought of it, too. "Nothing doing," he said.

"Are you that much of a coward?"

"Yes."

"But don't you know the ghost wouldn't come

around where there was light?" Thomas hoped that was true. "Besides, isn't it worth being scared silly if we find the treasure?"

Hal thought about that a minute. "Yes, I guess so," he replied.

Thomas walked carefully out of the kitchen with a lighted kerosene lamp, then headed for the shed. There he found a short-handled spade. On his way back toward the house, he thought he saw a flash of something white at the window of his old bedroom. Had a breeze blown the curtain, or were the girls spying on him?

The light from the lamp made it hard for him to see anything beyond its glow. *Oh, well, I'm into this now,* he thought. *No backing out now. . . .*

He got up under the house as fast as he could to keep the light from shining in the yard and betraying his presence.

Where's that Hal? He should've been here before now, he thought. Maybe he wasn't going to be able to sneak away. Thomas shrugged. Hal or no Hal, he was going to do some powerful digging this night.

Before he got started, he looked around carefully. The light shone brightly on the areas immediately near him, glistening off the pine timbers and sparking off spider webs hanging down around his head. Funny that he hadn't noticed them in the afternoon. Past the edge of the light, the wide spaces between the foundation pillars stretched like unending black caves.

Thomas jumped at the sound of movement in the

yard. Then he saw Coon Dog's face peering at him from just at the edge of the house.

"Come on, Coon Dog," Thomas whispered, patting his leg.

Coon Dog backed away in the sand. Suddenly, he wheeled around and started running toward the edge of the yard, growling and fussing.

Someone or something strange was coming. Coon Dog wouldn't be growling at Hal. Thomas didn't know whether to put out the light or to try to back out his side of the house and hide in the grove. Frozen in his place, he heard Coon Dog stop growling, and in just a minute Hal came crawling under the house.

That fool dog! And Hal was worse. "Hal, you're an idiot," he whispered angrily, not admitting to himself why he was so angry.

"I am, and we are," Hal whispered back, "and that's a fact."

"Well, anyway, now we're here. Let's get to work."

They went right to it, but it was slow going. They had to try to be quiet, and the one light they had forced them to dig real close together. It also meant they were in each other's way.

Thomas was trying to listen and to keep watch over his shoulder at the same time. "I can't help listening out for the haunt," he said.

"Me either, but I don't know what to listen for since I never heard him. Or felt him."

"He'll come at us a different way this time, I figure."

In that minute a sudden wind blew up from the bay

and raced past them, causing the light to waver and sputter in its chimney.

"What'd I tell you?" Thomas said. They both sat back on their haunches waiting for whatever might happen next. The wind blew like a whirlwind around the house, sending small twigs and leaves crackling around the yard, but this time not coming under the house.

Then suddenly it did and the lamp blew out.

Thomas clutched at Hal. "It's just a plain old wind," he whispered in the darkness. He'd never seen such darkness. He couldn't see his friend even this close to him. He couldn't see the spider webs or the pillars. There was just the darkness pressing close, smothering hot.

The wind had stopped as suddenly as it had started. From somewhere out in the yard, Thomas could hear Coon Dog growling softly.

"Which way is out?" Hal demanded, his voice sounding like shotgun fire.

"Be quiet, will you? Just follow the sound of Coon Dog's growling."

"Suppose he's growling at something bad?"

"It can't be worse than this darkness."

They had just gotten to the edge of the house when the door of the house was flung open and a light shone through.

Thomas kept crawling until he was clear of the house and then got up. Standing in the doorway was Mr. Parker looking ten feet tall. He came out on the porch holding the lamp high. Behind him came Thomas's mother and the girls.

"What in this world are you up to?" Mr. Parker demanded.

Thomas looked at his mother, but she didn't say anything.

"I told," Pearl said. "I saw you in the yard with a light, and then I saw you go under the house. That scared me so bad I couldn't go to sleep and I told." She sounded like she was apologizing a little bit, but mostly she seemed to be proud of herself.

"You took a kerosene lamp under the house?" Mr. Parker asked in astonishment.

"It's out now," Thomas said.

"I should hope so. Didn't you think of the danger of a fire?"

"No, sir. I planned to be careful."

Hal was sent home, the girls were sent to bed, and Thomas was told to wash up at the pump and come to the sitting room.

When he got there, they were sitting waiting for him, his mother in her gown and robe, Mr. Parker in his long nightshirt.

"Your mother has told me you believe there's a treasure buried under the house."

"Yes, sir, there is," Thomas said slowly. "My grandfather said there was."

"Your grandfather said an old sailor claimed there was," his mother corrected.

"Yes, ma'am."

"And you chose to dig for it secretly at night?" Mr. Parker asked.

"Well, I don't have time anymore in the day," Thomas said.

"But why make such a secret of this whole thing?" Mr. Parker demanded.

Thomas was too tired by now to try to make up a lie, so he just told the truth. "I was afraid you wouldn't want me digging under there. That's all."

"Humph," Mr. Parker said. "You're exactly right. I wouldn't. Such a foolish waste of time for a big boy like you." He took a couple of strides up and down the room. Then coming back to Thomas, he gave him a hard look. "And now, now after what you've done tonight, digging in the dark and what's worse—endangering the house and all of us in it by taking the lamp under there—I view the whole thing even more seriously. I'm going to have to forbid you to dig at all. At any time. Is that clear?"

"Yes, sir, but. . . ."

"No *buts*. Just let this be the end of it."

Thomas looked at his mother with wide eyes. How could she let Mr. Parker give him an order like that? It wasn't Mr. Parker's land, his house, or his treasure.

Thomas went up to her and caught her hand. Mr. Parker looked at him in disgust and left the room.

His mother shook her head. "It was a very foolish thing to do, son. And I was wrong to let you work at this secretly."

"But, Mama. . . ."

"I know, son, I know how you feel. But I think you must accept this punishment for now. And bide your time. Who knows? Things may change—they often do."

She walked him back to the kitchen door. "Will you be all right? I mean, you're not afraid out here?"

He grunted. "No, not now. That old haunt knows he can rest for a while now." He looked at his mother, still very angry. "But just for a while!"

Then without another word he headed for the stairs to the loft.

T E N

OLD MAN PARKER

Thomas pushed his broom awkwardly through the dirty sawdust around the icebox at the store. He was supposed to clear out the old wood shavings and replace them with fresh ones. He didn't like doing it. He didn't really like doing any of the jobs Mr. Parker had assigned him around the store.

Every day for two weeks now he'd come straight to work from school. Usually there were groceries to deliver to people's houses. Sometimes the counters or the glass cabinet fronts had to be washed down. Sometimes he straightened the bolts of cloth and lace over in the dry goods section. As soon as he finished one job, Mr. Parker had another one for him to do.

Life had suddenly become very boring. He couldn't dig, and there wasn't even any excitement in the loft at night. He hadn't seen, felt, or heard anything unusually lately.

Thomas was glad he hadn't told anyone but Hal about his earlier experiences with the haunt. Anybody else would say he was imagining things or lying. He wasn't lying, but—could he have imagined the snake's warning?

He was leaning on his broom when Marshal Vinson came in the door. Mr. Vinson had been a friend of Thomas's grandfather a long time before the town had elected him marshal.

"Howdy, Albert," the marshal said. "Howdy, Thomas." He helped himself to a couple of crackers from the barrel on the counter. Fishing in his pocket, he brought out a penny.

"Thank you, Marshal," Mr. Parker said, dropping the penny into the cash register. "Anything else I can help you with?"

"No, I just dropped in for a little visit. You folks heard about the big mullet run in the bay? Some say there's a school stretching a half mile long out there."

"Sounds like a tall tale or a long one to me," Mr. Parker said.

"It's not a tale at all. You ought to walk down to the water and take a look."

Mr. Parker rubbed his hands down his long white apron. "Oh, I couldn't do that. Couldn't leave the business. Besides, I'm not much of a fisherman."

"I am! I am!" Thomas cried. "Can I go see?"

"Well, no, Thomas," Mr. Parker said. "You've got work to do. And you've seen plenty of fish in the bay."

"Not that many. I'm nearly finished here," Thomas said evenly. "I could run down there and come right back."

"No, you couldn't, or wouldn't." Mr. Parker turned back to the marshal. "If there's nothing else I can help you with, I'll just get back to my work."

"Sure, sure. I'll be getting on now," Marshal Vinson said. "I'm going to round up my grandchildren and take 'em to the bay to throw the cast net a few times. Nothing better than fresh mullet." He turned to Thomas. "We haven't seen much of you around the water lately. The kids've been missing you. You trying to turn into a grown man overnight?"

Thomas didn't answer him. He had a feeling the question was really meant for Mr. Parker.

Marshal Vinson hitched up his pants and left in an angry sort of way.

Thomas tried with Mr. Parker one more time. "I'm nearly through here, Mr. Parker, Pa, sir. I could run over to the house for the cast net and catch us some prime mullet."

"No, Thomas, as I said before. And you might as well learn that I say what I mean and mean what I say. Now finish up quickly, and then bring your broom to the back of the store."

That evening when Mr. Parker went to the barn to milk the new cow, he took the girls with him. This gave Thomas a little while alone with his mother. Such times were pretty unusual these days.

She hugged him to her and brushed the hair out of

his eyes. "How's my big working man?"

He didn't answer her question, but blurted out his complaint, "How did he get to be the boss of me? How come you let him be the boss of me? He's not my father. He's not even my grandfather! And my grandfather was not ever so mean and hateful." He pushed away from her. "Why do all the good people die and the mean ones live?"

His mother got to her feet. "Hush, Thomas. I simply can't allow you to talk that way. Mr. Parker is not hateful or mean. He's just trying to teach you to work so you can make a living when you grow up."

Thomas threw himself in a chair and shook his head angrily.

"Son, son. We're very fortunate to have a good man who wants to be my husband and your father. And the little girls are trying so hard to be sweet and helpful. They want me to teach them how to cook and sew. Especially Pearl. She's very eager to learn."

"Pearl! Ugh, ugh, ugh! She ought to come down to the store and learn how to sweep. That's what her old man is teaching me."

"Thomas!" His mother frowned at him. Then putting a finger over her lips, she looked past him to the door.

Mr. Parker came into the sitting room from the back porch. He had washed his hands at the pump on the porch and was drying them with an old linen towel. The girls followed him in. When he was through with the towel, they fussed about who would be the one to hang it back up on the post outside. Thomas thought he might throw up.

"Thomas, I want you to get your wagon out and clean it up before dark," Mr. Parker said.

Thomas looked at his mother and scowled. She smiled nervously at him and nodded for him to go on.

He went, but he didn't get out the wagon. He sat by the shed door until it got dark. Then he slipped in through the kitchen and climbed up to the loft. Mr. Parker was not his boss. And that was final.

Thomas came out of a very deep sleep with someone's hand shaking him roughly by the shoulder. He stiffened in fear. The ghost had come back, this time in person.

"Up with you now, you scamp!" an angry voice said. It wasn't the ghost. It was Mr. Parker.

Thomas sat up, rubbing his eyes in the dark. "What—what are we getting up this time of night for? Is there a fire?"

"No, but I might put one on your backside if you don't get moving fast. You deliberately disobeyed me last night. I won't have that, and you might as well learn it now."

Thomas reached for his pants, remembering the wagon. It was still in the shed under layers and layers of dust.

"You're going to clean that wagon before school!" Mr. Parker ordered.

Thomas pulled on his shirt and pants and began edging toward the steps away from Mr. Parker. "I was planning to do it early this morning anyway. I must have overslept."

Mr. Parker was following him down the ladder. "A likely story," he said.

Coon Dog met Thomas at the back steps and followed him into the shed. When Thomas pulled the wagon out from the wall, Coon Dog put his paws up on it as if he might jump in.

Thomas shoved him away. "Move, dog. I got to clean this thing up. Old man Parker says what he means and means what he says."

Thomas was still sulking later that morning when Mr. Parker put a brown paper bag of sugar in a basket with six eggs and shoved it across the counter to Thomas. "Run this over to your Aunt Lena's house. She's needing this sugar in a hurry to bake a cake."

Thomas nodded, unhappy now with his aunt as well as with Mr. Parker. He'd seen her in the store just a few minutes ago looking at white blouse material in the dry goods section. Why couldn't she have carried those few groceries home herself? So he'd have to work harder, that's why!

He trudged down the sandy street toward the bay front, his bare feet getting very black. Mr. Parker had tried to make him wear shoes when he first started work. His mother had intervened for once, saying no one would expect a boy to wear shoes as hot as it was. He almost wished he had on shoes the second time he had to stop to pull sandspurs out of his heels.

Just before he got to his aunt's house, Hal came running up to him. His shirt front was bulging, and he had a mouth full of something. He spit two fat black plum seeds out on the sand and wiped off his mouth with the back of his hand. "Hey, Thomas. You working hard? How much money old man Parker paying you?"

Thomas scowled. "He ain't mentioned money. I'm probably working for the good of my soul."

"Your soul sure needs it." Hal pulled a handful of yellow plums out of his shirt front and bit into one.

"Look at who's talking!" Thomas dropped the basket to the ground. "And gimme some of them plums, you hog. Where'd you get 'em anyway?"

"Off Colonel Gillespie's tree. I just got my shirt full when his cook come out and run me off with her broom." He handed Thomas a fistful of plums.

The two boys chewed and spat for a while in satisfaction.

"Hey, Thomas. Pa says the bass are thick down at the point today. Hurry and get rid of those groceries so we can go fishing."

Thomas thought a minute. He would like to do just that. Seemed like a year since he'd wet a hook. Then he shook his head. "I got to finish the day out," he said slowly. "Why don't we go after supper?"

"We could, but we'd better take your boat. Ours is leaking like a mosquito net."

Thomas hesitated. "Mr. Parker said I wasn't to take the boat anymore without his permission. He'd probably say no just to keep in practice. We'll take yours and bail when we need to."

"It'll take a lot of bailing."

"Then, we'll bail, you lazy boy." Thomas picked up

the basket again. "Hey, Hal. You been down to the railroad track lately?"

Hal nodded. "Just about every day."

"How far have they laid the tracks?"

"Nearly to town, Thomas. You want to go see?"

Now Thomas was really tempted. He could take Aunt Lena her stuff, they could run down to the track for a couple of minutes, and he could get back to the store before Mr. Parker hardly missed him.

"Let's go!" he cried.

ELEVEN

BROKEN EGGS AND A LEAKING BOAT

Thomas and Hal ran almost the whole way to where the men were laying track out past the edge of town. Part of the way they had to push through heavy underbrush under scraggly pine trees. The land hadn't all been cleared yet for the track's roadbed.

Once there Thomas wiped the sweat out of his eyes and stood happily watching the men at work. He'd like to stay here all day, every day, dreaming of the time when real locomotives came charging down these rails into Sarasota.

Some of the men working on the track were tall and heavy-set, and some were lean as young pine trees. But all of them were strong and black. The sweat ran down from under their straw hats or head rags and glistened on their faces. Their muscled arms moved in rhythm, up and down, up and down, driving the long

▲95

spikes through the holes in the tie plates.

They sang as they worked, a kind of chant that matched the moving of their arms:

"There ain't no hammer. . . ." *Pow!*
"On this a'heah mountain. . . ." *Pow!*
"That ringa like mine boys. . . ." *Pow!*
"That ringa like mine. . . ." *Pow!"*

In just a minute Thomas spotted Sample moving along the side of the track with a wooden bucket. Whenever the men reached a stopping place, he was quick to hand out gourds of water, which they poured down their throats and over their faces. When Sample wasn't quick enough, the men yelled at him angrily and called him names.

Thomas watched, wondering if he or Sample had the most menial job. The work crew reached for their hammers again, and Sample ran over to where Thomas and Hal were standing.

"Hello and good-bye," he said. "I got to get back to the barrel for more water."

The foreman was a white man. He yelled louder than all the rest, "Hey, you water boy! Get your lazy bones to movin' before I break a few of them!"

Sample moved his bones, and Thomas decided he'd better move his.

When Thomas got back to the grocery store, Mr. Parker pulled his watch out of his pocket and looked at it very crossly. "It took you an awfully long time to deliver that small order. Has your Aunt Lena moved up to Braidentown?"

"Uh, no, uh, no, sir." Thomas fished in his mind for an excuse to cover the situation. Had he really been gone all that long a time? He couldn't think of an excuse, so he began making up a lie. "You see, my aunt had run out of stove wood, and I stopped to chop some up for her in a hurry." That sounded pretty good, so he went on. "Then I filled her wood box back of the stove. You know she hasn't got a boy to help her now since Sample is working at the tracks."

"Hmmm. I didn't know chopping wood was a skill of yours. I'm surprised."

"Oh, yes, sir, my grandfather taught me when we camped out."

"I hope all this is true."

"Oh, yes, sir." A little of it was, the part about his grandfather. And the preacher had given him and Hal a few workouts at the woodpile, too.

"All right then, but you'll have to stir yourself to finish your work here. I want you to scour the back steps. There's still blood there from the butcher's delivery."

"Yes, sir. Right away."

"That is, if you're not too tired from chopping wood."

"Oh, no, sir."

Pumping water into a wooden barrel, Thomas began to feel very uneasy. Mr. Parker didn't act as if he believed him.

97

Sample and I have about the same kind of job, he thought. *One thing for sure, though. When that old train starts running, I'll have me a way to get away from this place. In a hurry!*

In the late afternoon Lucy served supper on the back porch next to the kitchen. It got pretty hot with the sun bearing down like some kind of a round furnace. On the porch there was almost always a cooling breeze.

They sat at a long oak table with two benches along the sides and a straight wooden chair at each end for Thomas's mother and Mr. Parker.

Thomas's mother passed him the rice and then the black-eyed peas cooked with chunks of salted white bacon. "Take some more, son. You haven't eaten enough to keep a bird alive."

She always said that, although they both knew he ate enough to feed a flock of hungry buzzards. But tonight he hadn't really eaten much. He was eager to get through and go fishing with Hal at Five Points. Besides that, he had an uneasy feeling the lies he'd told this afternoon were going to come back to haunt him. He didn't yet know how, but as he took another spoon of peas to please his mother, the how arrived on the back steps.

Aunt Lena had come to call.

"Evenin', Lena," his mother said. "Come have some supper with us." Mr. Parker got up and offered her his chair.

She took it and said she'd already eaten her supper but would have a cup of coffee.

"I hope that cake you were going to bake turned out just fine," Mr. Parker said.

Aunt Lena looked at Thomas with a scowl. "Well, I didn't get to bake it. Two of the eggs Thomas brought over were cracked, and I never use a cracked egg. I should have broken the other ones on that scallawag's head."

The girls giggled but hushed when Thomas shot them a fierce glance.

"That's a shame, Mrs. Tisdale," Mr. Parker said, clearly annoyed. "First thing tomorrow he'll bring you some more. Early enough for breakfast if you like."

"No matter," she said, sipping at the steaming hot coffee Lucy had put at her place. "I couldn't have baked the cake anyway. I was too low on firewood. Marmalou's home with the croup today, and Sample's at the tracks. I came by to see if Thomas here could come over after supper and chop some wood for me. Young scamp owes me a favor. Don't you, Thomas?"

Thomas almost turned over his bench getting up. "Sure, I will, Aunt Le–Lena," he stuttered. "I'll go right now."

Mr. Parker's face was just about as angry as a summer rain cloud. "Just a minute, Thomas," he said. "I think you and I have something to talk about."

Thomas groaned inside. Not here in front of everybody! "Yes, sir, I—I know we do. But I'll have to hurry to fill the box 'fore dark. I'll come back soon as I finish."

Before Mr. Parker could say another word, Thomas was off the porch and on his way.

In Aunt Lena's backyard Thomas propped one piece of wood against another, preparing to give the wood a wallop with the axe.

All the time he was running over here he'd been trying to think. He'd known from the minute his Aunt Lena had exposed his lies that, treasure or no treasure, he was going to run away again, but he was afraid not to chop the wood first. He was even afraid to go by Hal's and tell him he couldn't go fishing.

The main thing was that he was afraid. Afraid to face Mr. Parker.

Where should he go? Would Hal go with him? Maybe together they could fend off the wild men and the renegade Indians in the woods.

He worked long enough to fill the box half full and then took a chance on going to Hal's. Maybe the preacher and his wife were off visiting somebody.

Hal was sitting on the front steps with his cane fishing pole, looking madder than Coon Dog when a cat jumped him. "Where've you been? We've plum missed the tide."

"I can't help it. I'm in bad trouble with Mr. Parker, and I'm going to run away. You've got to come with me."

Hal shoved his fishing pole away and stood up. "Me? Run away this time of day, with no reason at all?"

"Because we're buddies, that's all."

Hal sat down again. "Even if you're my buddy, I'm scared to do it. I've never run away before like you have."

"Ain't nothing to it. You just get on the road and go."

"I don't know. I got to think about it."

"We don't have time to think. We got to go while we've got some daylight."

"But where?"

"I think I have a good idea. There's a place we can go and live like men with nobody to boss us around. Come on, bring your pole and the bait. We're going to be eating a lot of fish. We'll have to take your boat, too."

"We can't get far in that leaky thing."

"We'll get far enough," Thomas said.

They started toward the bay, walking fast but not running. They didn't want to attract attention.

Hal's old boat was tied to a stump near the pier— one end on the sand, the other in the water. There were several inches of water in the end that was floating in the water.

Thomas ignored Hal's worried look and motioned him to start pushing the boat off the bank. Bending over to push, Thomas was startled to see a pair of small hands grab the rim of the boat beside his.

Indigo! That crazy Indigo. She was throwing her thin weight against the boat and pushing as hard as she could.

Thomas pried her hands off the boat and shoved her away. "Just what do you think you're doing?"

"I'm helping you get the boat in the water," Indigo said.

Hal had stopped pushing at the boat now and stood

back, staring unhappily at Thomas and Indigo.

"How did you know we were down here?" Thomas demanded.

"I followed you from the house over to Hal's. I heard everything you said."

"You little sneak," Thomas said.

She tossed her head, her chin stuck out a mile. "I don't care what you call me. I figured you were going to run away again. I thought I might go with you."

The boys stared at each other now, their mouths wide open.

"You can't do that," Hal said.

"Why not?"

"Because you're a girl. Girls can't run away with boys."

"Why not?"

"Because it's not right, that's why not. And besides, we don't want you. What good would you be?"

Indigo's chin dropped a bit. She looked down into the boat. "I could bail."

"No, you couldn't, because you're not going," Thomas said. "And you're just ruining everything. Go home. Come on, Hal. Push."

Indigo was still standing there, watching them. She looked little and skinny and sad. For just a second Thomas was sorry he'd spoken so hatefully to her. But he dropped his head and got back to work. "Push, Hal. Can't you push?"

As quick as a flash, Indigo leaned over the boat and began pushing with the boys. With the three of them leaning and shoving against it, the boat finally slid off the bank and floated onto the softly bubbling water at the edge of the bay.

Indigo jumped in and started bailing.

"We told you you couldn't go," Hal said, nervously.

Indigo shrugged and kept bailing, scraping the can across the bottom of the boat and pouring the muddy water out over the side. The edge of her long dress was wet up to her knees, but she didn't seem to care.

In a moment she straightened up. "I don't want to go. I just want to help you get away. I can't stand the sight of either one of you anymore."

She jumped out of the boat to the bank, balancing herself by catching hold of a cedar branch hanging over the water. Then she turned and faced them again. "Thomas, your evil ways are about to catch up with you. You fooled around with that fan long enough to draw some of the curse. You're probably going to get out in the bay, and this boat is going to sink clear to the bottom."

She said it as if she hoped it would happen. Reaching down, she gathered her skirt between her fingers and squeezed out some water. Then she wheeled around and ran toward home.

Hal had been listening to her with his mouth open. Now he turned toward Thomas. "What's she talking about? What curse?"

Thomas shrugged his shoulders impatiently. "No curse. It's something silly I made up to scare the girls. Come on now, will you?"

Hal backed away. "Naw, Thomas. She's ruined it all. She's a curse herself. She'll go tell that we've gone. Pa will come and whomp the devil out of me." He picked up his fishing pole and the bail can. "Come on. Let's go home."

Thomas snatched the pole out of his hands. "You go on home. You're nothing better than a girl. I'll go by myself." With that, Thomas began rowing and soon found himself out from the shore a little way. Then he headed the boat south. It would take some powerful rowing to get down the bay and then across it to the key before dark. One thing in his favor was that it always seemed lighter on the water. He might make it if he didn't have to stop too often to bail water out of the boat.

He'd be lucky if he didn't run into some nosy fisherman who'd want to know why he was out alone this time of evening. On the other hand, if he got into real trouble with the boat, it could be handy to have a fisherman nearby. Curse or no curse, a leaky boat wasn't the best way to cross the bay at night.

Thomas had only a vague idea of where he was going. He'd never been to Billy Muldoo's camp, having only heard about it. The only people who actually went there were looking for devilment. At least that's what folks said. Thomas didn't know all the ways grown people got into devilment. He knew from the preacher's sermons that demon rum was mixed up in a lot of it.

Thomas wasn't looking to get into any devilment. He just wanted to live free like Billy Muldoo on Sarasota Key. The way to start was to find Billy. Before it got pitch dark.

The wind was picking up in the bay. Small waves broke against the boat, forcing Thomas to row harder to keep on course and make headway. He could handle the waves if they didn't get any bigger, and he didn't mind the salt spray in his face. What he did mind was the water beginning to lap around his ankles inside the boat.

It was impossible to bail and row at the same time. Hal should have come to help. Thomas rowed on a minute. Hal was right to stay. It was crazy to be out here in this boat.

Thomas stared at the mainland, which had become only a black smear against the blacker sky. Glancing across his shoulder, he thought the key seemed closer. He had to try to reach it.

If he could get there, he could pull up on the beach and bail out the boat. Then he'd follow the shoreline to the first bayou running back up through the middle of the narrow island. Billy's camp was supposed to be somewhere on the bank of that bayou. Hopefully, Thomas couldn't miss it.

Thomas rowed hard. He was afraid to stop to bail for fear the current and wind would carry him farther away from the key. His arms ached. He had never rowed this much in his whole life, and never had the bay seemed so awful big.

TWELVE

OLD DEMON RUM

Indigo took her time going home. She was really angry with the boys and didn't want to have to smile and be polite around the family.

"They're hateful. That's what," she whispered in the growing dark. "Who wants to go on an adventure with them anyway?"

By the time she'd gotten to the gate, her anger had changed into worry in spite of herself. Suppose the story about the curse was true and Thomas had drawn it?

She ran then into the house and to the sitting room, where her father was reading the paper and her step-mother was helping Pearl with her embroidery. They looked very proper in the soft lamplight. For the first time Indigo was conscious of her wet dress and muddy hands.

Her father peered at her over his paper, eyeing her

dress. "Why, Indigo, look at you! Where have you been and without permission, I might add?"

"I know, I know, and I'm sorry, Papa."

She twisted her hands together, trying to decide how much to say. She didn't want to tattle, she truly didn't, but Thomas might really be in danger on the bay.

She didn't have to decide. Hal had slipped into the sitting room and was standing there with a red face, looking as miserable as she felt.

Thomas's mother put aside the embroidery and stood up, a worried expression on her face. "Where's Thomas?"

"Well, I'm just not sure," Hal answered, "but when I left him, he had started across the bay in our old boat."

"At this time of night?"

"Yes, ma'am. And I wouldn't have told you, but the boat is leaking bad. My pa's not at home, so I thought I better come here."

"Oh, that boy! Oh, that boy!" Thomas's mother cried, starting to run from the room.

Mr. Parker jumped up from his chair. "Where are you going, Olivia?"

"To get Hooper. He can go after Thomas."

Mr. Parker caught her arms. "Now why are you getting so upset? Thomas has probably turned around and come back to shore by now. He knows all about leaking boats, doesn't he?"

"But you just don't know how stubborn he is. He may not turn around." Her eyes flashed in the light. "I'm going for Hooper."

He held her tight. "No, dear. You stay with the girls. I'll go for Hooper, and the two of us will go after Thomas. Don't worry. If he hasn't come back with the boat, we'll go right out on the bay after him. He can't have gotten far."

"Ohhh, that's what I'm afraid of," Thomas's mother cried.

Indigo went up and caught her arm. "Let Papa go, please. Let him go before it gets any darker."

She nodded her agreement then, and Mr. Parker released her and turned to Hal. "But where was he headed? In which direction should we look?"

Hal's chin dropped. "I—I don't know. He only said we'd go live where we could catch fish. That could be anywhere."

It had grown very dark by the time Thomas reached the bayou. He felt safer out of the wind from the bay, but not very much. He rowed slowly, peering between the trees for some sign of Billy's camp. He expected to find a dock with boats and up on shore a house of some kind. This early in the evening Billy ought to be up with a kerosene lamp burning, making the house easy to see.

But there was nothing. Nothing except dark branches hanging out over the water and tall trees standing up against the sky. Occasionally there was the crash of something along the shoreline. It could be a log falling or an alligator awakened by the noise coming out to see what was disturbing his bayou.

Frogs and crickets tried to outsing each other. Mosquitoes swarmed and buzzed at Thomas's ears and stung every bare spot on his body. Every now and then a bird added a long wail to the chorus around him.

He rowed and stared, growing more and more afraid. He had started praying off and on, as soon as it'd gotten full dark. It hadn't helped. *Maybe God doesn't listen to boys who run away,* he thought mournfully.

Thomas pulled deeper on the oars. Of course God listened to runaway boys. It was part of his job as God. He listened to runaways and all other kinds of sinners. The preacher had said so. There was a secret in it though. Something about being sorry and promising to do better in the future.

"And that's just what I'm going to do," Thomas whispered in the darkness. "If I can just find Billy's camp, I'm going to start doing a lot better. I'm going to work hard catching fish and smoking them to sell and make money. And when I get a little older, I'm going to Tampa and ship out on a freighter to the China Seas and make my fortune. I'll send my mother money for whatever she needs."

He slapped at the mosquitoes swarming at his ears, nearly losing an oar in the dark water. Catching it firmly again, he added, "And I might even send the Baptists some money so they can build a church like the Methodists did."

Thomas let out a groan. He didn't know which part of him hurt the most. He had to find Billy's camp soon!

He smelled the camp before he found it—smoke and hot fish! It was close. It had to be.

In just a moment he saw a dock. Not a real dock, but a dark mass of fallen trees and roots jutting out into the bayou, with a couple of boards wedged in among them.

He nosed his boat into the crazy dock, dropped anchor, and scrambled up on the unsteady boards. In a few steps he was up on dry land. He didn't know exactly where he was or what to expect next, but for the dry land he was truly grateful. "Much obliged, God," he whispered.

Following the smell and the smoke, he made his way through the underbrush until he came to a narrow shed under the trees. Smoke drifted out from around its door. Inside there would be fish smoking over a low bed of coals.

For the first time Thomas remembered he'd eaten almost no supper. He felt starved! He was tempted to help himself to some fish, but decided he'd better not. He'd find Billy first and at least introduce himself.

Staring into the dark trees, Thomas spotted the outline of a small house and one dimly lit window.

"Mr. Muldoo, sir," he called. "Mr. Muldoo?" He moved toward the house, but no one answered his call.

The house was really only a shack with a tiny, sagging porch. The whole thing leaned crazily into the trees. Thomas stumbled over the front steps, righted himself, and made it up to the door. "Mr. Muldoo?" He knocked timidly, worried a little now about how the old man would react to a runaway boy showing up on his doorstep.

There was no sound from the shack. Thomas

pushed on the door, which made a scraping noise across the floor and opened just wide enough for him to get inside.

The reason he had seen only one lighted window was because there was only one window. An oil lamp stood on a table made of planks stretched across saw-horses. Several old kitchen chairs stood around—one minus a leg. Lying all over the floor were dozens of mostly empty cans and liquor bottles.

A pile of old quilts occupied one corner, and on top of the pile was Billy sound asleep, his head stretched back, his eyes tight shut, his mouth open. An empty bottle rested in one outstretched hand, and part of the contents of the bottle had soaked the front of his filthy shirt.

Old demon rum has gotten hold of Billy for sure, Thomas thought.

Suddenly Billy snorted and shifted his position on the quilts, making the bottle slide out on the floor at Thomas's feet. Thomas backed up and sat down on the edge of one of the chairs that had all its legs.

Thomas looked around the room again. It didn't look exactly the way he'd pictured it, and it smelled worse than the back end of a livery stable. He shrugged unhappily. Maybe Billy would look better in the morning.

Thomas got up and went back outside. The fresh air made him feel hungry again. He'd just have to eat some of the old man's fish and square it with him somehow later.

He walked over to the smokehouse. The burning

coals inside gave off a dim light. Thomas picked up two smallish fish by their crisp tails and nudged the door shut with his elbow.

In the shack he put his fish on the table and sat down, then glanced over toward the pallet. Billy was gone.

Thomas shrugged and lit into the fish. He would worry about Billy later.

Olivia paced up and down in the sitting room. Then stopping in front of Mr. Parker, she stamped her foot against the floor. "I just can't believe you found him and then went off and left him! In that terrible place, with that old reprobate!"

"Now, Olivia dear, it's not such a terrible place," Mr. Parker said, trying to soothe her feelings.

All the way back to the mainland from the key he'd worried over her reaction to his going off and leaving Thomas on the key. He'd expected her to be upset, but he hadn't even known she possessed such a temper.

"It's just a dirty fish camp," he continued. "Thomas was sound asleep on a pallet when we found him. That really riled me up.

"I'd gotten sick with worry by that time. We'd rowed all up and down the shoreline to see if he'd beached the boat. When we didn't find the boat, Hooper said he figured Thomas had headed to Billy's camp. Then we had the bay to cross, worrying all the way. And when we found him, he was sleeping as unconcerned as Coon Dog taking a nap under the big oak."

"Where was that dreadful Billy Muldoo?"

"Out fishing, I expect."

"Was there anybody else about?"

"Not a soul. I'm sure he's quite safe."

Mr. Parker wasn't as sure now as he had been on the key. Hooper hadn't wanted to leave Thomas, but Mr. Parker had insisted the boy needed a lesson. There was no better way for him to learn the drawbacks of running away than to stay a day or two in that dirty shack with very little to eat. Still, he certainly didn't want to put Thomas in any danger.

He patted his wife's back consolingly. "Don't worry now, dear. If you like, I'll send someone for him first thing in the morning. I can't go, of course, because of the store. Right now he's fine. What could possibly happen to him tonight?"

Mr. Parker took comfort in his own words. What indeed could happen in a quiet fish camp in the middle of the night?

Thomas woke to the sound of shouts and laughter coming from the woods around the shack. Every now and then there was a crash as if someone had fallen into something or somebody. Then there'd be loud groans and curses. Maybe this was the devilment people talked about when they talked about Billy's camp.

Easing up to the window, Thomas shaded his eyes against the glass and looked out. A bonfire burned down near the dock. In its light he could see men moving among the trees.

Thomas heard someone crash against the front steps, then stomp across the porch. He whirled to face the door just as a huge man lurched through it.

The man was not only big, but fierce-looking, with flashing black eyes, coal black hair, and arms the size of elephants' trunks. His loose white shirt fell down over tight black pants cut off just below his knees. A black scarf was knotted around his bulging Adam's apple. Two gold teeth glittered in the front of his wide mouth.

"Madre, mia!" the man cried. "An accursed *niño! Qué pasa?* Has Señor Billy found a son?"

Thomas's mouth dropped open. Was the man a sailor from one of the ships that traded between Cuba and Tampa? Sometimes they stopped off in Sarasota to swap rum and tobacco for oranges. Maybe Billy had his own trading business.

The man really looked like Thomas's idea of a pirate, but of course, there weren't any pirates around here anymore. At least, Thomas hoped there weren't any pirates around here anymore!

When the man moved toward him, Thomas backed away. However, the man came fast, grabbed him by his arm, and began pulling him out of the shack.

On the porch the man stopped. "Halloo, Señor Billy! I found your *hijo.*" He shook Thomas like a sack of rags. "You want to trade him to me? I take him to Cuba to work the cane fields. He bring me good money."

Two or three other men had stumbled up to the

edge of the porch. One of them sang out a long paragraph in Spanish that Thomas couldn't understand, then translated into English, "No, no, Señor Guillermo. Let me sell him to the mill. He can be a mule— pushing the grindstone."

The men all laughed then, but it didn't sound like a fun kind of laughing. It was more like the kind boys did when they were up to some kind of real meanness. Coming from these big men, it was downright scary.

While Thomas was struggling to pull away he saw another figure move up the steps. He recognized Billy's flapping beard and felt some relief, but the relief didn't last long.

Billy gave the sailor holding Thomas a thump on the back and waving a bottle in Thomas's face, cried, "How much will you give me for him?"

Thomas fought even harder to be free. "I am not for sale!" he protested loudly.

Billy put his bottle down carefully against the wall and pried the man's hands off Thomas's arms. Then catching him firmly himself, Billy turned back to the sailors. "How much will you give me then? How much in a decent trade?"

They all laughed again. Thomas tried desperately to break away, but Billy began dragging him into the shack. Shoving him across the room, he pushed him down on the pallet.

"Keep quiet and out of sight now. Guillermo would as soon cut your throat as sell you. He's the curse of these waters. Don't you know that?" With a final glare, Billy stepped out the door and pushed it shut.

Thomas curled up in the corner, trembling. He hadn't known it. He hadn't even known there was a Guillermo. Did Guillermo's being a curse have anything to do with the curse of the fan? Thomas shook his head reminding himself he'd made up the whole story about the fan. As scared as he was right now, though, it seemed as if it weren't even a lie.

From outside he heard more shouts and laughter. Once or twice he heard, *"niño"* and knew it meant him. A lot of times he heard, *"aguardiente,"* which he thought meant rum.

He tried to think what he could do. Could he slip out to the boat and row away? No, not likely. The men were all around the smokehouse and the dock. And even if he could get past them, the plagued boat was probably full of water by now.

There was one chance. If the men got drunk enough, they might go to sleep. He could bail the boat out then and get away.

He waited for what seemed like hours, but the ruckus outside didn't seem to be dying down much.

In spite of his fear he felt tired and very sleepy. Maybe he should take a little nap. That would give him the strength to row hard and fast. It was going to take more energy to escape than he had right now. He turned carefully on his side with his back to the wall.

Phew-ee. It was the second time he'd lain down on these old quilts tonight, and they smelled worse this time than the first. His stomach churned as if it might be getting ready to throw up the fish.

He had never in his life felt so miserable and afraid.

He tried to tell himself he really had nothing to fear from the loud-mouthed sailors. But, if he had nothing to fear, why had Billy snatched him away from Guillermo and shut him up in the shack?

He eased onto his back, trying to get his nose a little further from the quilts. He thought of his clean straw pallet at home—it seemed fit for a prince. And compared to Guillermo, even Mr. Parker looked pretty good.

"O Lord, just let me be safe and let me sleep. I'm ready to face up to my punishment for lying and running off. I'm really going to try to stop all that. I'm going to try to get along better with Mr. Parker, too. Just, please, Sir, help me get home."

THIRTEEN
BILLY MULDOO

Thomas woke up early the next morning when a bright shaft of sunlight sliced through the window into his eyes. He sat up straight, prepared to do some kind of battle.

But there was no one around to do battle with. Everything was quiet in the shack and outside. He scrambled to his feet, then bent stiffly to scratch his legs. These new welts looked and itched like flea bites.

He was hungry, but more than that he was thirsty. He hadn't had any water to drink last night after the salty fish. There wasn't anything to drink in the cabin now, except the scummy-looking dregs in the scattered bottles.

He moved over to the window and looked out the dirty pane. Oaks, cedars, and pines grew close together around the shack and spread their branches over its roof. Vines and palmettoes matted together in a thick underbrush among the trees.

Thomas pushed the door open carefully, half expecting to find a heap of men passed out on the porch. The porch was empty and, as far as he could tell, so was the camp. Only the wild cries of the birds flying over the thickets broke the silence.

Thomas walked all around the shack looking for a pump, but the only water he could find was collected in an old barrel. The barrel was splayed open and splintered around the top. Thomas cupped his hands in the water and drew some out. It was clear except for some leaves and a couple of bugs floating in it. He smelled it and took a small taste. It was water all right, sweet rainwater. Dipping his hands in several times, he drank until he wasn't thirsty anymore.

There was still no sign of anyone. Thomas ran down the path to the bayou. This was the time to get away.

At the dock he stopped suddenly. He wouldn't be getting away in the boat. It had sunk clear to the bottom. Thomas could see its rim glowing whitely up through the murky water.

That Indigo! She'd put the hex on it. Thomas enjoyed feeling angry with her for a minute, then shrugged off the idea. The sailors had probably sunk it deliberately.

"Hateful scum!" Thomas said out loud.

An egret startled by his voice lifted her long white wings and flew over his head.

Thomas spotted another small boat tied up to a stump near the dock. It was probably Billy's, and

Thomas wasn't about to mess with that, not unless he got really desperate.

No matter about the boat. Now that it was daylight he could cut across the key to the gulf beach. Sooner or later someone would find him. Nothing seemed as scary this morning as it had last night. Maybe he had dreamed the sailors and their threats.

Thomas looked around. Wooden racks in a small cleared space were draped with casting nets. A huge tree had fallen halfway into the water and braced itself up on broken branches. Its wide trunk had been whittled flat to make a kind of table. Dried blood and fish scales stuck along the edge of its surface and down the sides of the trunk. No doubt, this was where Billy cleaned his fish.

Two huge pelicans joined Thomas, their wingspread shading the table as they coasted over it. They perched on the branches in the water, their long bills hanging down in front of their chests like storage tanks. They eyed Thomas expectantly, waiting for him to clean some fish and toss the entrails in the water for their breakfast.

"Shoo, shoo," he said crossly, waving his arms. "Go catch your own fish." They only withdrew their heads a little, staring at him with great haughtiness.

"What's that? What's that you say?" A gruff voice spoke from the other side of a clump of mangroves.

Thomas caught his breath, but after a moment's hesitation he made his way to the bushy trees. Cautiously, he pushed through the branches and found himself in another small clearing.

All he saw was a pile of rotting boats covered with vines. Then there was movement at the bottom of the heap, and Billy Muldoo came crawling out. "Can't a man get no sleep at all?" he fussed.

Billy looked nearly as bad today as he had last night, but not as scary. His old clothes hung about him as if they'd been thrown on a rack. His hair, a mass of gray, red, and straw-color, hung down and curled into his beard. His light blue eyes were red-rimmed; his nose was streaked with red. His shoes were so huge and bulky Thomas figured he had made them for himself out of deer hide.

When Billy moved toward Thomas, Thomas stepped back. He wasn't really afraid, but he didn't want to get close to the old man.

"Don't be trying to run off now, laddie," Billy said, still moving toward him. "There's no place for you to run anyway. Your boat's at the bottom of the bayou. Lucky for you you ain't with it, or et up by alligators."

Thomas backed into the mangrove trees. "I—I'm just on my way to the beach, or maybe around to the bay side. I'm going to wait for someone to come fishing or swimming. They'll take me back to the mainland."

"Well, sure they will. If they spot you. And if you find the beach in the first place. Pretty thick swamps along this shoreline. And thick woods to work through to get over to the gulf."

He caught Thomas's arm and pulled him back to the boats. He sat down heavily and pulled Thomas down beside him.

▲121

Billy then peered into Thomas's face. "Why would you want to go back? You're a runaway, ain't you?"

"How—how did you know I was a runaway?"

Billy pursed his thin old mouth. "By the age of you. By the clothes on you. By the flesh on your bones. You've not the look of a bum off the boats or out of the woods. You've been eatin' regular, you have, and takin' a bath on Saturday night." He peered at Thomas again. "Ain't that right, boy?"

Thomas hung his head. "Yes, sir."

"And from the shape of your boat I figure you lit out from Sarasota. You couldn't have made it from much farther than there."

"That's about right," Thomas hedged, not wanting to give away too much information.

"And when you came here last night, where did you think you'd be going next in that old tub?"

"I wasn't going from here. I was going to stay, at least for a while."

Billy's eyes widened in astonishment. "Stay? Here? Do you think I want a little youngun here, snifflin' and mewlin' about and gettin' in my way?"

Thomas jumped to his feet. "I'm not a little youngun. And I don't mewl and sniffle. I was going to fish like you do and smoke mullet. And when I'd made some money, I was going to buy a good boat and go far away. Very far away."

Billy pursed his mouth and shrugged his shoulders. Then he leaned his head back against the boat. He was quiet so long Thomas thought he'd gone to sleep, but after another moment he opened his eyes again. "Well, you got a fair plan. I could use a smart boy around the place. You could wash the nets and hang 'em to dry. You could clean fish. You could scrape barnacles off the bottom of the boat."

This was beginning to sound like pretty hard work to Thomas. Still, it was more a man's work than sweeping out the store and carrying eggs to cross old ladies.

"Now if you're bound to stay, you better scour out the cabin right away," Billy continued. "Your ma wouldn't want you living in a sinkhole the likes of that one." Billy nodded his shaggy head, agreeing with himself. "If it's cleaned up, it ain't gonna be so thick with fleas when the weather gets hotter."

Thomas gulped and nodded. More fleas. And the shack getting hotter and hotter when they moved into deep summer. He was liking his plan less and less.

"Do you want to see my little house?" the old man asked.

"Your house? Don't you live in the shack?"

Billy scrambled to his feet. "No, sirree. Except in the worst of storms and the coldest part of winter."

"Well, where is your house?"

The old man looked astonished again. "Right here, of course," he said, waving one ragged arm grandly to cover the heap of rotting boats.

Thomas's jaw dropped again.

Half angrily Billy pushed him down to his knees and gave him a shove. Thomas crawled in, remembering that the old man had crawled out from under the boats.

The boats on top of the pile had been angled upside down to cover one large boat lying on its bottom on the sand. Billy had lined worn wooden planks across the seats of the bottom boat to make a sort of floor. Crawling up on those planks, Thomas was a foot or more above the sand, with another foot or more of uneven headspace.

The air flowed in a cooling stream between the spaces formed by the angled boats above his head. At the bow a triangle of space provided a view of the bayou running black and calm between the rushes and trees growing thickly along its banks. Every few minutes a sleek cormorant hit the water, diving for fish.

Thomas stretched out on his stomach and watched the birds. He sighed deeply. What a neat hideout this would be. But a house? A permanent house?

Billy pounded a fist on the boat's side. "Come out of there now. Move smartly."

Thomas came out.

"And you're not to go in again, d'you understand?" Billy half growled. "I only showed it to you to give you an idea of what you could make for yourself when you've worked a year or two. You have to pay me off first, of course. Last night I traded off a lot of work to get that Guillermo off the island."

Thomas sat down in a hurry. "Was he really here? And the other men? I thought maybe I dreamed it."

"They were here. First time for Guillermo since he broke out of the brig in Cuba. He'll likely be back though. Says something of his is buried in Sarasota."

"Really?" Thomas was so fascinated with the whole

idea of the big sailor he forgot to be afraid. He got up on his hands and knees and moved close to Billy's face. "Really?" he asked again. "A treasure maybe?"

Billy pushed him away. "Oh, who knows, or takes the risk of knowing?" He rubbed his rough hands over the tousled mass of hair on top of his head. "Oh, my poor head. I caught a wicked blow last night from one of the boys." He glared at Thomas. "And don't ask me, 'Really?' again." He sighed. "Guillermo'll be back, or somebody like 'im, every night or so. Most times from your own Sarasota. Not much sleep to be had around here, m'boy."

Then laying his head back against the boat, Billy closed his eyes.

Thomas waited as long as he could to ask him a new question. "Mr. Muldoo, how long you been living here?"

Billy opened his eyes and scratched his head. "I dunno exactly. I forget. Thirty, forty years. Since sometime after the Civil War."

Thomas nodded. "Folks say you deserted. . . ."

A sharp blow to the side of his head cut him short.

"I never, never deserted!" Billy was leaning over him, staring with a fierce expression.

Thomas put his hands over his ears just in case another blow was coming.

Billy seemed satisfied with Thomas's attitude and sat back against the boat. "I mustered out, I did. A'course I did it my own way, without all them officers and their fine papers. I just left. The war was over and I left." He glared at Thomas again as if he were expecting a quarrel, but Thomas didn't say anything. He didn't want another hit on the head.

"And I didn't go back home. No use doin' that. My pa wanted to apprentice me to a pharmacist. That's why I ran away and joined the army in the first place. No use goin' back home."

"But, Mr. Muldoo, didn't you ever get homesick? Didn't you miss your family?"

Billy shook his head again. "I forget. I think I got homesick, but I didn't have the money to go back. I wouldn't go back penniless, you know. Or I had the money one time or another, but then I wasn't homesick." He fished around with his hand up under the boat and pulled out a bottle. He took a long drink and then sat staring out over the bayou. In a moment he said, "Maybe they never wanted me back."

He sat upright suddenly, scowling at Thomas. "You talk a powerful lot. I don't know as I can stand a youngun around talkin' more than a dadgummed mockingbird."

Thomas sat up straight himself. "I'm not—I don't—."

"Och, and it's time for you to go to work. It ain't fittin' that you be lollygaggin' about like a sick raccoon. Get to work on the cabin, and do a good job of it or I'll be beatin' the daylights out of you."

Thomas scrambled up to his feet. "Can—can I have breakfast first?"

"Breakfast? What would that be? I forget." He scratched his head. "Some kind of eatin' I'm thinkin'. There's only fish here, and later in the summer, berries." He waved the bottle at Thomas. "A'course, there's always rum. Here, have a dram."

Thomas backed away. "No, thank you, sir. I'm not a drinking man myself." He moved backward into the mangroves, then righted himself and crawled through. Stopping at the crazy dock, he stood staring at his sunken boat.

Thomas felt sick with disappointment. Billy was just a drunken old bum. And maybe a mean one. He didn't have a free and wonderful life. Thomas knew if he lived here, he wouldn't have one either. Exciting and dangerous maybe, but certainly not free.

Thomas looked down the bayou at the thick trees and at the vines and bushes growing right in the water. It wouldn't be easy to fight his way through all of that to get back to the pass. And it wouldn't be any easier to swim across the bayou and go through the woods to the gulf. He could do it though, if he could just stay straight and not go around in circles.

If, if, if. If he got to the beach safely, and if somebody came along with a boat. If they'd take him across the bay so he could go home.

Tears filled Thomas's eyes and began rolling down his cheeks when he thought of the biggest *if* of all. *If* his family wanted him to come home.

He brushed the tears away half angrily. No matter, he was leaving this place now! He grabbed a handful of branches, thinking to wade down in the water to test how shallow it would be here along the edge.

Then he froze. The creak of oars sounded clear

from just down the bayou. Who was coming? Guillermo? Why?

Cautiously he parted the branches, watching for a boat. Then, all caution aside, he pushed out of the bushes and scrambled down onto the dock. Pulling deeply and steadily at the oars was the preacher. Somehow Thomas knew the preacher was coming for him.

FOURTEEN
JUDGMENT DAY

As soon as the boat bumped against the crazy old dock, Thomas climbed in and sat in the prow behind Brother Watson.

In a moment Brother Watson said, "Well, hello to you, and why don't you come sit where we can see each other? Makes it easier to talk."

Thomas wasn't sure how much talking he wanted to do at this point, but he clambered over the middle seat where Brother Watson was sitting and flopped down on the wide back seat as he'd suggested.

Brother Watson held the boat up against the dock with an oar pressed down into the mud. "Do you think you ought to tell Billy you're leaving?"

"Oh, I 'spect he knows I'm leaving," Thomas said hastily. "He's probably watching from behind those mangroves. Let's just go on."

But go on where? The place he most wanted to go was home. He wanted a bath even if it wasn't Saturday. He wanted some of Lucy's biscuits and a cold drink of sweet milk. And he wanted his mother to forgive him and keep on loving him. He wanted his stepfather to give him another chance.

Thomas looked up from under his eyelashes at the preacher, who had turned the boat around and was moving it out into the current in the middle of the bayou. He waited until the oars were rising and falling in a steady pattern, sending the boat smoothly down the water. Then he burst out, "Do you think they'll have me back?"

Brother Watson stared at him, surprised. "Have you back? Of course, they'll have you back. You're their son, aren't you?"

"Yes, but I thought. . . ." Thomas fell silent, hoping against hope the preacher had it figured right. Then from nowhere suspicion and anger stirred in his mind. "How'd you know where I was? That Indigo told you, didn't she?"

"Well, she didn't know where you were going, but she and Hal did tell us you'd gone."

Thomas's good feelings completely melted away. "Hal! He's supposed to be my best friend!"

"He is. That's why he told. Indigo's your friend, too. They got scared our old boat might sink and you drown. Mr. Parker and Hooper started out looking for you right away."

Thomas was astonished. "I didn't know old man Parker would even get in a boat!" He thought that over for a minute and added, "Anyway, they didn't find me."

"Yes, they did. You were asleep in Billy's shack. Mr. Parker decided since you wanted to be there so badly he'd let you stay awhile."

Thomas had to think that over, too. Mr. Parker surely hadn't let him stay to make him happy. There had to be another reason. Probably he thought Thomas would get sick of the whole thing in a hurry. Which was exactly what happened.

Thomas leaned over the boat's edge and looked down into the water. They had moved out of the bayou and over the shallow flats of the bay. Through the clear turquoise-colored water Thomas could see fish darting through the weeds, feeding, or just getting out of the way of the moving oars.

He looked up to find the preacher watching him as if he were waiting for another question. Thomas had one. "Why did you come after me? Why didn't *he* come back?"

"Oh, he had the store to mind, and then he wanted me to talk with you about the way you've been acting. Which hasn't been very good." He looked back over his shoulder to get his bearings and then back at Thomas. "Why did you run off, Thomas, this time?"

Thomas scowled. "Because of Mr. Parker, of course. He doesn't like me at all. And he won't even let me dig under my own house. Me and Hal used to do that all the time, and nobody cared." He splashed one hand down into the water, sending the spray flying. "Why did God have to make stepfathers anyway?"

"Maybe because he knew we would need them to fill in for natural fathers from time to time." He rowed in silence for a moment. "Have you tried to do anything to make him like you?"

"No. Except working at the store. But nothing I do suits him. Just because I broke two eggs. . . ."

The preacher looked at him, then stared out at a circle of bubbles left by a leaping fish.

Thomas sighed. "Besides, I lied to him. I lied because Hal and me went to watch the men laying track, and I was late back at the store. I knew he'd have a fit so I lied."

Brother Watson nodded. "Thomas, did you ever think about the fact that lying itself is a kind of running away?"

"It is?" Thomas had never thought much about lying at all. He just did it.

"Think about the reasons people lie. Why you lie." He stared at Thomas. "Well?"

"You mean think about it right now?"

"Why not! We've got nothing else to do for a while."

Thomas scratched the bites on his ankles and legs and thought. "Well, like yesterday I lied because I was scared of what would happen if I told the truth. I guess you could say I was running away from what might happen."

"Uh, huh, that's right."

Thomas trailed his fingers through the water. "I lied when my grandfather died. I didn't want to go to the funeral, so I said I was going home to feed Coon Dog. Instead I hid up in Grandfather's attic."

"Were you trying to run away from sadness?"

Thomas nodded, his face turned away. "But just

before the funeral my Aunt Lena came up in the attic for something, and she spotted me. I had to come down and go to the church after all."

"Well, that's the way it goes, son. For whatever reason you run away, you always have to come back."

"Billy didn't. He really ran away and he never went back."

"That's true."

Thomas shaded his eyes with his hands and peered toward the mainland to see how far they had to go. He knew now that Billy hadn't come out ahead for all of his running away. He had pretty much messed up his life. Thomas wasn't ready to admit that to the preacher or anybody else right now.

He could see the pier and the buildings on it. He hoped Brother Watson would beach the boat on the shore near his house and not go down to the pier. He wanted to get home without anybody seeing him and maybe laughing at him.

"We're almost there," he said, with a sigh. He twisted in his seat, wanting to ask something else, but also hesitating to. When he couldn't stand it any longer, he blurted out, "What do you think Mr. Parker will do to me?"

"I don't know," Brother Watson said. "But whatever it is, you have to face him and your punishment." He pulled strongly at the oars, sending the boat shoving up into the soft sand at the edge of the shore. In another few minutes he was tying up at a broken-off stump of a tree.

Thomas started climbing out of the boat, but the

preacher caught his shirttail. "One more thing I want to say to you."

"Yes, sir?"

"Thomas, you've got a fighting spirit in you—and a fiery streak of independence. Some see that as bad, but I don't. I see it as a possible strength. Somewhere along the line you're going to have to decide whether to use that strength for good or bad. You can be a strong person, a leader, on the right side or the wrong side. It's your choice. Do you understand?"

"Yes, sir, I think so," Thomas said with a sigh. He was too hungry and sleepy to think much of choices right now. Then he caught hold of a branch and pulled up onto the shore. Turning back to the preacher, he said, "Yes, sir. And thank you for coming after me. Hal's lucky. You're a nice kind of father to have."

Embarrassed then at what he had said, Thomas turned quickly and started running up the sandy path toward home.

By some kind of miracle his mother was home by herself. She grabbed him in a fierce hug and then just as quickly shoved him away. "Thomas, how could you do this to me? Don't you know I've been worried sick?"

He hung his head. He hadn't really thought how she'd feel. "I didn't think, Mama. I was just so scared of Mr. Parker I ran away."

"Scared of Mr. Parker? But, Thomas, why? He's never laid a hand on you."

"I thought—I thought he'd work up to it."

She frowned. "Be that as it may, you shouldn't have lied. And then made everything worse by running away. Thomas! What are we going to do with you?"

"What are you going to do with him?" Thomas demanded. "He's the one that caused it all."

She shook her head at him. "Thomas, your stepfather may have been too hard on you, I'll grant you that, and I think he will, too. But you didn't just start lying or running away when he came. Now, did you?"

This made Thomas so angry that he thought for one second he'd just turn around and take off again. Only for a second. He was too tired and hungry. Besides, his mother was right.

The promises he'd made to God when he was on the water and in the camp came flooding back to him like a high tide. He twisted in his place. He wasn't used to taking much blame when he was in trouble or apologizing either. But promises to God were pretty important.

"I can—can do better," he finally stammered. "And I will."

Her face brightened with a smile, and she looked as if she might hug him again, but she didn't. With her face serious again, she said, "You know you'll have to be punished. We can't just act as if nothing happened yesterday and last night."

"I expect to be punished," he said. "It's only fitting."

Then she gave him a hug.

Late the next afternoon Thomas stood staring glumly at a cord of split logs heaped next to his barn. He figured he would be a grown man before he ever got the whole pile chopped up small enough for firewood and stacked as Mr. Parker had directed.

He was to work at the job for an hour every day after he came home from the store, with no break except Sundays, until the job was finished. It was a better punishment than getting a daily thrashing until he was grown, but not much better.

Thomas picked up the axe and hefted it in his hands. There was one way he'd grow, for sure. Chopping a whole cord of wood would give him some sizeable muscles.

And he didn't think he'd run away again for a while. It wasn't just his promises to God. Right now it seemed that it was hardly worth the effort.

He hadn't worked more than fifteen minutes when Indigo appeared. She stared at him a few minutes, then disappeared into the shed. *Hateful girl. Probably going to hide in there and spy on me through a crack in the wall,* he thought.

To his surprise she came out again, dragging an axe behind her. "I'll help," she said matter-of-factly.

Thomas glared at her. "Why would you want to help me? You hexed my boat and it sank."

"No, I didn't. I only said it could happen. And I was sorry after. I prayed for you, Thomas. I prayed you'd be safe."

Thomas kept his scowl intact. He didn't really want her praying for him even if it had worked. It only meant he owed her a favor.

He shrugged and turned his back on her. "Anyway, you don't know how to chop wood," he said.

"You could teach me."

"Why should I?"

"If you don't have some help, you're not going to get to go fishing or hunting for a long, long time. And you might even miss seeing the train when it comes in."

The train! She was right. He was very likely to miss seeing the train on its first trip into Sarasota. If it came during store hours or wood-chopping time, he'd just be out of luck.

"Well," he said hesitantly. "If you're determined." He picked up a piece of wood. "You have to lean one log against another like this." He bent down and demonstrated. "Then you have to lift the axe up high, and pow! Hit 'er smack on the end."

Indigo scurried to arrange a pair of logs as he had. Then she grabbed her axe handle and lifted it up over her head. She grinned at Thomas and brought the axe down with a bang. It caught the very edge of one log, which went flying in the air and left her sprawling.

"Lawd! Lawd! Lawd!" Lucy cried, running down the steps and through the yard toward them. Her eyes were wide, her full skirts flying. "Gimme that axe, chile! You want to cut your foot plumb off?"

"I'm learning to chop," Indigo said, getting to her feet.

"No, you ain't no such thing. Ain't no girl in this house going to chop wood," Lucy said firmly.

"But I want to!"

"Don't matter. Your pa's goin' to skin you, for sure.

Worse than that, if you gets hurt, he'll kill Thomas. Go on in the house now. Lay the supper table or play dolls with Pearl."

Indigo's mouth quivered. She looked at Thomas and back at Lucy. "You can't talk to me like that."

"Well, Missy, I done did." Lucy took the axe out of Indigo's hands and put it back in the shed. Then she tromped indignantly back up the steps and into the kitchen.

Thomas felt relieved that Lucy had put a stop to Indigo's wood-chopping lesson. At the same time he felt that he ought to apologize for the way she'd done it.

"Don't mind her," he said. "She's been bossing me around since I was born."

Indigo tossed her head. "When I am grown, I shall do just as I please."

Thomas nodded, though he didn't really believe her. He did want to make her feel better. After all, she had tried to help him. "For a girl you have big muscles," he said.

"Humph," she answered, tossing her head again. She started walking to the house, then turned around and gave Thomas a half smile.

Thomas wondered what she'd think if he told her about what had happened to him on the island. Especially about the fierce sailor who had to be some kind of pirate.

Later at the dinner table, he had started to tell the whole story, but Mr. Parker was so outdone he'd hushed Thomas up with one of his "let-that-be-the-end-of-it" orders.

Still and all, Thomas had an idea Indigo would like to hear about his adventures—all of them.

FIFTEEN
THE TRAIN

Hardly a day went by that someone didn't come into the store talking excitedly about the new train. When would the last section of track be laid? Would the railroad company build a fine new station? Thomas liked to say the whole name of the company—United States and West Indies Railroad and Steamship Company. It sounded mighty important.

This would be the first train since the old Slow and Wobbly. Colonel Gillespie had built that one to run between Sarasota and Braidentown. Thomas didn't remember it, but he'd heard about it so much he felt as if he did.

Colonel Gillespie's train had earned its nickname for very good reasons. It had run on rickety rails laid out most of the way on bare sand. The locomotive had been an old, second-hand wood burner that pulled two flat cars. Passengers sat on plank benches on one car with only a canvas canopy to keep off the sun and rain. Once or twice the whole train had fallen right off the tracks.

The new train would be something else. It would have a newer wood-burning steam engine, a real day coach, a Pullman to sleep in, and a baggage car.

Thomas got so excited when he thought about the new train he could hardly keep his mind on his work. One day Mr. Parker gave him a sharp rap on the head with his knuckles. Two ranchers were in the store, and trying to listen to them made Thomas idle too long.

Thomas resented the rap on the head, but he busied himself with his dust cloth, edging along the counter close to the men. They'd come in for chewing tobacco and were talking about how many of their cows the train might knock off the track.

Thomas didn't want to miss any conversation that had to do with the train.

"Some say she'll pull into town in another two weeks," one of the men said. He unfolded a long, lean knife and carved himself a chew from his plug of tobacco.

"The train will be the making of this town," Mr. Parker said.

"Or the breaking." The cattleman sounded half angry. "I don't cotton to seeing the town all overgrown with strangers. First thing you know they'll want to pave Main Street so them visiting ladies can sashay between the hotels without getting their skirts dirty. Next thing they'll be hollering that we got to fence in the cows."

Thomas giggled behind his dust cloth. It wasn't just the ladies visiting in the hotels who complained. His mother and aunt were always fussing about how carefully they had to step on Main Street!

"Thomas! You've about rubbed the varnish off that counter," Mr. Parker complained. "Why don't you get a clean cloth and dust the glass on the cabinets?" He looked back at the cattlemen, who were rolling out the door with the gait of sailors home from the sea. Then he looked back at Thomas. "I, for one, would like to see Main Street paved, even with crushed shell. It would certainly help keep the shops clean."

"Yes, sir," Thomas nodded. "It sure would."

Thomas was determined to please Mr. Parker if there was any way to do it. He wanted to get on his best side so that when the train came in, Mr. Parker would let him off work to go see it. He might do better than that.

Looking up at his stepfather, Thomas spoke carefully. "Will you close the store and go see the train when she pulls in?"

"I doubt it," Mr. Parker said. "Trains are nothing new to me. Besides, that should be a good day for the store. People will be downtown in force, excited. They might even spend a little extra money."

He gave Thomas a serious look. "You have to learn things like that, if you want to be a successful merchant."

"Yes, sir," Thomas said and bent over the glass to hide his face. *A merchant!* Not in a million years. And he wouldn't do what Billy did either. He'd join the army and stay in it, or the navy. Maybe he'd even be the engineer on a train!

But right now, he'd just polish this glass. And anything else Mr. Parker told him to do.

The day for the arrival of the train finally came. Thomas went to work happy and excited but came home late that afternoon angry and frustrated. He flung himself in the porch swing, sending it flying sideways almost against his mother's rocker.

"I knew it would happen like this!" he cried. "I knew it!"

His mother put down her darning basket and stared at him anxiously. "Thomas, what's going on? Where's Mr. Parker? Supper's been laid by for ages, and the girls have already gone on to the station to wait for the train. Is there something wrong at the store?"

"No! Just a whole lot of extra work. Mr. Parker probably planned it that way. He knew the train was coming in this evening, and he still let that wagon come in for a delivery right at closing time. We had to unload the whole thing. Then he told me I still had to chop wood for an hour!"

"Oh, dear, surely not in this case. . . ."

Thomas began to cry. He hated himself for it, but he couldn't seem to help himself. "He said no exceptions. Not now. Not ever."

He put his hands over his eyes and rubbed them, trying to stop crying. At the same time he was glad his mother had seen him do it. She ought to know how miserable he was. He peeked through his fingers to see how she was reacting and saw instead that she was looking toward the street.

"Your stepfather's coming home," she said, getting up from her rocker. "Poor man. He looks exhausted."

"Poor man!" Thomas cried, outraged.

"Thomas, you go quickly and eat your supper and then get straight to the woodpile. Perhaps if you show a good spirit and work hard, he'll make an allowance just this once."

"He won't. I know he won't." Thomas wiped his face off quickly on his sleeve, hoping Mr. Parker hadn't glimpsed him crying. He jumped up and ran straight through the house and out to the woodpile. For once in his life he wasn't hungry.

Thomas reached for his axe and leaned a log against the chopping block. He gave it a sharp blow with the axe just right, and the log split neatly in half. Then he sighed and leaned on his axe. Why was he trying so hard? Mr. Parker wasn't going to relent. He wasn't the relenting type.

He glanced up when he heard Hal come charging into the yard, yelling as he came. "Hey, Thomas! Why are you still messing around here? I been looking and looking for you. Folks are already gathering. Come on now, or you're going to miss everything!"

Thomas shrugged miserably and wiggled the head of the axe into the soft sand. "I can't go yet. I gotta do my hour. Old man Parker said so."

Hal's mouth dropped open and his eyes flashed fire. "And you're going to mind him? Just like that? And miss the train? Come on, Thomas, we been waiting for this train practically all our lives."

Now Thomas was angry with Hal. "What can I do? I'm telling you he said I had to work today just like every day!"

"Do? Do what you've always done before. Just take off and go. What can he do about it? He can't kill you. He probably won't even beat you because of your mother."

That was true. Thomas had the feeling Mr. Parker had just about pushed his mother too far. He could leave. He really could. Or he could work until his mother and Mr. Parker had left. Then he could sneak away, see the train, and run back without any of them being the wiser.

Except him. He would be the wiser. He would be back into that old lying and cheating stuff. Did he really want that?

He gripped the axe handle hard. "No, Hal. I can't go. I just can't. You go on now. I mean it. Get on out of here."

Hal shook his head in disbelief, but Thomas lifted the axe and began to chop. Without another word his friend ran out of the yard.

Thomas felt tears welling up in his eyes again, but he fought them back. His punishment was too hard. It was just too hard.

He continued chopping at a steady pace for a few

minutes and managed to stop crying. Then he heard someone coming across the back porch and down the steps.

That's probably Mr. Parker, Thomas thought. *He read my mind awhile ago and is coming to warn me to stay on the job. How can I ever get along with a man like that?*

"Thomas, hold on there a minute," Mr. Parker said. Thomas looked up at him. "Your mother says you're very upset at missing the train."

Thomas looked away.

"Now, Thomas, you know I'm a man of my word, and as such I can't break my word about the hour of wood chopping."

"But why did you take the delivery?" Thomas burst out. "If I hadn't had to work late, I could have made it fine."

"It was necessary. The wagon was due back in Tampa by noon tomorrow. The men will get very little sleep as it is."

Thomas shrugged unhappily. What Mr. Parker said made sense, but it didn't help as far as missing the train was concerned.

"Seeing the train means so much to you then?"

Thomas shrugged again. If Mr. Parker didn't know how much it meant, there wasn't any way he could tell him.

"Well, then," Mr. Parker said. "We'd better look sharp."

Thomas raised his head. Mr. Parker stepped past him and went to the shed. He came back carrying an axe. Then picking up one of the heavier logs, he laid it on the ground a little way off from Thomas, as if he were setting up another chopping block.

Mr. Parker pulled out his gold watch and studied it briefly. "It is now ten minutes after seven. If we each chop wood for a half hour, that will account for the full hour you're supposed to work. Perhaps you will still have time to get over to see the train come in."

Thomas's mouth dropped open.

Mr. Parker put his watch back into his pocket and frowned at Thomas. "Well, what are you waiting for? Get to chopping."

Without a word Thomas did just that.

As soon as Mr. Parker looked at his watch and said, "Time's up," Thomas dropped his axe and took off running.

He stopped at the gate, knowing he hadn't done exactly the right thing. He ran back to the woodpile, threw the rest of the chopped wood onto the stack, and then ran to the shed with his axe. He could go now, and he did, without even glancing at Mr. Parker.

At the little railroad station he spotted Hal and Sample up in a tree near the track. He ran to the tree, put a bare toe in a knothole, grabbed the stub of a broken limb, and hoisted himself up beside them.

Hal grinned at him. "Decided to come, huh?"

"Well, not in the way you think," Thomas panted, trying to catch his breath. He still felt angry with Hal somehow, but he was too excited to start a quarrel over it. "Y'all hear the whistle yet?"

"No, but Sample put his ear down to the track a minute ago, and he said that old train is on its way."

Thomas wiped the sweat off his face with his shirt sleeve. "Can you truly hear it that way, Sample?"

"Sure you can. The crew boss told me so, and he know all about trains."

Thomas eased his back against the trunk of the tree and stared out into the dusky evening air. There! There it was. He heard it for himself. A distant rumble like thunder at the end of a summer day. A thin, drawn-out wail of a whistle strung out through the air.

"Here it comes, here it comes!" All three boys shouted at once. A nearby group of townspeople raised a cheer. The ladies clapped their hands and waved their fans.

Thomas saw smoke rising above a clump of trees and heard a louder rumble. The black engine charged into view. Then it slowed and screeched to a stop, brakes grinding, just on the other side of where the boys were sitting.

The engineer leaned out the window of the cab and waved to the crowd. Behind him the fireman waved a red handkerchief over the engineer's head. In a moment the conductor jumped down off the step of the day coach and began helping passengers down.

Thomas and his friends tumbled down out of the tree. Then Thomas and Hal pushed their way past the adults standing close to the train and broke through right next to the engine. Sample had skirted the crowd and now eased up to join them again. "Ain't she a wonder?" he said in awe.

"The prettiest thing I ever saw," Thomas said. Then he raced down along the train to the caboose and back up to the engine again, elbowing aside anyone who got in his way. Full of excitement, he ran his fingers along the gleaming wet metal of the cab. Then he shook the cow catcher at the front, wondering if the shiny frame was really strong enough to shove a cow off the track.

The engineer had come to the window of the cab again. He leaned out looking over the crowd, then down at Thomas. "Hey, boy, you want to come up in the cab?"

Thomas gasped. "You mean it? Me? Hal and Sample, too?"

"Sure. Why not?"

Thomas hardly felt the metal step as his bare feet went up into the cab. The engineer stepped back, waving grandly at his proud domain.

Thomas admired everything he saw—the throttle, the firebox, the chain to pull the big brass bell, but his eyes kept going back to the throttle.

The engineer grinned at him. "Why don't you take hold of it for a minute?"

Thomas eased his hand around the throttle, then stretched his body and leaned out the window as the engineer had done. He felt full grown and very powerful.

Hal nudged him hard. "How about giving me a chance?"

Thomas shoved him away. "Wait a minute, will ya?"

The engineer stepped up. "Whoa now, none of that in my cab. You boys take turns."

"Me, too?" Sample asked quietly.

"Sure," the engineer said. "Why not?"

Thomas moved aside reluctantly to give way to Hal, then went to the window on the other side of the cab and hung his elbow out. He leaned back against the frame, dreaming of the time when he could be a real engineer. He'd go flying down the track like a northeast wind to somewhere far away—Georgia or even Virginia.

A few people were moving through the sandy lot on the side of the train, still admiring it. At the edge of the trees, half hidden behind a tall pine Thomas saw a tall man shift his weight. Thomas stared at the huge, dark figure and then drew back in astonishment. It was Guillermo.

Later when he was home, Thomas lay on his straw pallet in the loft, too keyed up to go to sleep. This had turned out to be just about the best day of his life. The roaring beauty of that train coming down the track, the sound of it, the smell of it, the feel of the throttle in his hand—it was all so big in his mind there was almost no room for anything else.

Almost. A couple of other things kept getting in the way. Guillermo, for instance.

It surely had looked like Guillermo behind the tree. And Billy Muldoo had said Guillermo was coming back to Sarasota to dig up a treasure that belonged to him.

A wild possibility struck Thomas. Was Guillermo's treasure the same one that was buried under Thomas's house? Guillermo certainly looked like the big black-haired sailor described in the old story.

Thomas shook his head in the darkness. It just couldn't be true. There must be hundreds of dark-haired sailors in these parts. And lots of different treasures, too.

He fought to put the whole thing out of his mind. He probably hadn't even seen Guillermo. Even if he had, what the ugly man was or wasn't looking for didn't matter. Thomas had nothing to do with Guillermo anymore.

Thomas rolled uneasily to the other side of the pallet. There was someone else he did have to deal with.

Why had his tongue gotten so tied up when he'd come home tonight? Why had he stood in front of his mother and Mr. Parker, hanging his head in silence as if he had no tongue at all?

His mother had tried to help him. "Thomas dear, now that the girls have gone to bed, isn't there something you'd like to say to your stepfather?"

Thomas had felt a wave of embarrassment flood over him. He'd twisted in his place, drawing circles on the wooden floor with his toes. Without looking up, he'd finally said, "Wasn't the train something? Wasn't it a sight?" He looked up then, almost at Mr. Parker but more through the middle of him.

"Yes, dear, it was a sight," his mother had said. "And what else is there for you to say?"

Thomas had dropped his head and drawn some more circles.

After a moment Mr. Parker had said, "Never mind, Olivia, dear. Don't prompt him. He must work a thing like this out in his own mind."

Thomas's mother had sighed deeply, making Thomas feel worse.

"Well, to bed with you!" Mr. Parker had grumbled. "We've got a great deal of work to do tomorrow. Trains come and go, but work is always there."

"Yes, sir," Thomas had said before giving his mother a hug and his stepfather a quick glance. He'd left the sitting room in a hurry.

Now he was beginning to feel really miserable again just remembering the scene. He hadn't needed any prompting. He'd known exactly what he ought to have said to Mr. Parker.

He ought to have said, "Thank you. It was a good thing you did for me when you helped me chop tonight's wood." But he hadn't said it, and he didn't think he could say it tomorrow either.

Thomas sat up on the pallet. It was too hot to sleep up here tonight. He decided to get some citronella from the kitchen to fend off the mosquitoes; then he could curl up in a quilt on the back porch.

He was easing out the kitchen door when he saw Mr. Parker standing on the porch by the pump. The soft moonlight gleamed on his long white nightshirt and on the white porcelain washbasin under the mouth of the pump.

Thomas stood very still watching as Mr. Parker thrust both hands into the basin water and dashed it across his face, along the back of his neck, and on his hair. *He must have gotten hot, too,* Thomas thought. Mr. Parker shook his head like an old dog. Then, taking a towel hanging on a nail over the pump, he rubbed himself dry. He stood for what seemed like a long time staring out across the yard.

Thomas took a silent step back into the kitchen, afraid he would be seen when Mr. Parker turned around. After a moment, Thomas peeked out again, but Mr. Parker was gone. Thomas sneaked onto the porch and stretched himself out along the floor next to the center hall door.

He hoped never to be this unhappy again in all his life. Why couldn't he have just stepped out while the two of them were alone and said, "Thank you, Mr. Parker, Pa, sir"?

Instead of doing that, he had run away, not off to the woods or the key, but off somewhere inside himself. Away from Mr. Parker.

Thomas curled up in his quilt. If it had been his own father, he could have said the words right off. Then he had to admit something else to himself. Mr. Parker had acted like a real father this afternoon.

Thomas stared straight up at the ceiling of the porch and forced his mind back to the train. It had been a wonder—a true wonder.

SIXTEEN

THE SECRET

For the next few nights Thomas managed to get down to the tracks every evening to see the new train finish its run into the station. He made it there on time by skipping supper and getting right to his job at the woodpile.

And every time, he felt the same wondrous excitement that he had had the first time he'd seen the train charge into view, brakes grinding. He loved its delicious smell of steaming wet metal and burning wood.

It wasn't only the train that brought him to the station. Each evening, no matter how excited he was, he found himself staring over at the tree where he'd seen Guillermo hiding the night the train first rolled in.

He couldn't forget Guillermo—the size of him or the flashing of his gold teeth. He couldn't help wondering about the treasure Guillermo was looking for. Had he maybe found it and left, or was he still looking?

And most important of all, was Guillermo's lost treasure the one hidden under Thomas's house? "I better not catch him fooling around my house!" Thomas said out loud and then looked uneasily over at Guillermo's tree again.

Tonight was special. Thomas wasn't going to the station. He was finishing up the wood-chopping job, and he was doing it ahead of schedule. Once he'd made up his mind he had the job to do, he had worked like a mule, not asking any time off either.

He stacked up the last of the splintered logs neatly, then stood back to admire his work. Even with Lucy burning up a lot of it in the cookstove, there should be enough to last them into the winter.

He put the axe in the shed and came out into the light, and examined his hands. They were not as tanned as they used to be when he spent most of his time loafing in the sun, but they were lean and strong. The blisters that he'd gotten at first had given way to thickened skin, and his back and arms were stronger. He straightened himself, proud of how strong he was, not just from the wood chopping but from lifting boxes and things at the store.

Thomas didn't know exactly what he was expecting out of his family when he went in and told them he had finished. It was a special time to him—it ought to be to them.

Especially to his stepfather. He'd laid out the job, hadn't he? He ought to be able to brag on Thomas for once. He might even let him start looking for the treasure again.

Thomas took another look at the stacked wood as he passed it and walked around to the front porch where the family was sitting.

His mother was working on what looked like a dress for one of the girls. The material was full of little flowers, certainly not for him. Mr. Parker was sitting in the swing, reading the paper. For once his tie was loose, his shirt open at the neck. The girls were playing jacks on the wide bottom step. Thomas stepped past them, putting down an impulse to accidentally knock the jacks off into the sand.

As he passed, they stopped playing and put their faces down in their hands, giggling as if they had some kind of secret. When he stood in front of his stepfather, he said, "Well, I'm done."

Mr. Parker looked up. "You're done with what?"

"With chopping the wood. The whole stack," he said with a great deal of satisfaction.

"Oh." Mr. Parker looked back down at his paper. That seemed to be all the comment he was going to make.

Thomas felt his sense of pride fading away. His mother was bobbing her head at Mr. Parker as if she were telling him to go on and say something else. But he didn't.

Thomas shrugged his shoulders, then started off the porch without looking at any of them.

"Just a minute there," Mr. Parker said. Thomas turned back. Mr. Parker had folded his paper and was staring at him. "You don't expect me to compliment you on concluding a punishment assignment, do you?"

"Come now, Albert, dear," his mother said. "He's done a very good job. Give him that."

"He has indeed. He's an excellent wood chopper. I do compliment you on that, Thomas. And on your faithfulness to the task once you settled into it."

"Yes, sir," Thomas said, feeling embarrassed with the compliment even though he'd wanted it.

"I think the wood chopping should be your chore from now on. Hooper's getting too old for such heavy work."

"Yes, sir," Thomas said again, not too happy at the turn the compliment had taken. "But we won't need any more chopped before next winter."

"That's good. It'll free you up for some other work that needs doing around the place. You could begin to clear a garden for Hooper to put in some vegetables when fall comes."

Thomas almost groaned out loud, but stopped himself. "But I was planning to catch up on my fishing, beginning tomorrow."

"After you've done your work, of course. Work comes first," Mr. Parker said.

"Albert, you do beat all." Thomas's mother bit off a thread with a snap. "You're tormenting the boy, and the rest of us, too."

Mr. Parker looked at her in surprise. "Why, I wasn't meaning to do that at all. We were just having a man-to-man talk about work."

"Enough talk about work," she said. "You'll spoil the . . . evening."

The girls were giggling again, and Thomas wished

he were anyplace in the world except right here.

"Did you put up the axe?" Mr. Parker asked him.

"Yes, sir, it's in the shed."

"Well, I'd like you to go put it in the barn. The shed's begun to leak. I want all the tools stored in the barn until I can get the shed roof mended."

Thomas sighed. "All right, sir. I'll do it now."

He started down the steps and the girls jumped up. "Can we go watch? Can we?" they begged their father.

"No," he said. "Let the boy alone."

Thomas walked back to the shed to get the axe, then headed toward the barn. Mr. Parker had to be the pickiest, strictest man who ever lived. And he wasn't going to live with him, not much longer. Even God couldn't expect it of him.

He pulled open the wide, creaking door of the barn. The first thing he saw in the soft evening light was his wagon. That was strange. The wagon stayed down at the store now that he was hauling groceries in it.

Thomas drew a sudden, deep breath, and then for a moment he couldn't breathe at all. A beautiful little horse was hitched to the front of his wagon.

As if he were in a dream, he eased his way around the wagon to get a better look. She was a soft, rich brown with a large creamy spot across her back. Her big eyes fixed themselves on Thomas, and she gave a nervous whinny.

"Whoa there, little girl," he whispered. "Don't you fret now. I wouldn't hurt you."

He came up close to her and passed his hand gently down her back. When she didn't move, he eased in closer and rubbed the top of her face and the place between her ears.

"My, you're a pretty baby," he said. The little horse didn't seem afraid of him at all now, and he put his arms around her neck. "How did you get here? Why are you hitched to my wagon?"

She whinnied again, and Thomas laid his face against her neck. He had the wildest hope that maybe he knew the answers.

He eased back from the horse. "Just a minute now, little girl. I'm going to go find you some sugar. You'd like that, wouldn't you?"

He backed out of the barn, closed the door, and bolted it.

"She won't go away," Mr. Parker said.

Thomas wheeled around and stared at his stepfather.

"She's beautiful," Thomas said. "She's little, too. Is she just a baby?"

"No, she's what they call a Shetland pony. She won't get much bigger."

"But how—where—who's—?" he stammered.

"She's yours, Thomas."

"Ohhhhh," Thomas breathed out a great sigh.

Mr. Parker had almost been smiling, but now he looked his old stern self again. "I knew when you started school again you'd have a hard time keeping up with your work at the store and the chores around the house, too. I thought the horse would help you in delivering groceries. It's good for the business to keep things moving smartly along."

"Oh, yes, sir," Thomas cried. "Very good for the business."

"You'll have to take care of her, of course. She's your responsibility."

"I will. I will."

Mr. Parker nodded. "Now, maybe you'd like to go get that sugar."

"Oh. Yes." Thomas was so excited and so happy he was having a hard time breathing again, much less speaking. But there was one thing he knew he wanted to say. "And thank you. I really thank you."

Mr. Parker cleared his throat. "It's nothing. As I said, it's good for the business."

"Yes, sir." Thomas didn't care about that. The horse was good for him.

Mr. Parker said something else in a low voice.

"Sir? I didn't understand you."

Mr. Parker cleared his throat again and swallowed. "I said—I just said that I always wanted a Shetland pony. When I was a boy, you understand."

Thomas nodded. He didn't understand everything, but he understood a little. Not knowing what else to do, he reached out, grabbed Mr. Parker's hand, and shook it furiously. Then he turned and ran for the kitchen.

When Thomas came back out with the sugar, his mother, the girls, Mr. Parker, and Coon Dog were all out at the barn looking at the pony. His mother gave him a hug, and the girls jumped up and down all around him, clearly happy about the new addition to the family. Coon Dog hadn't yet made up his mind how he felt. He lay on the ground with his head between his paws gravely watching all the excitement.

"Settle down, girls," Mr. Parker said. "The pony is used to children, but she's new here and may feel a little uneasy."

"Did they ride her?" Thomas asked, eager to try riding her himself.

"No, she was trained to pull their wagon. That's why I thought she'd be good for you. You might try riding her later on, after she's used to you."

Thomas nodded. He wanted to take her right now over to Hal's house, but the girls were so excited he didn't think it was right to run off with his treasure. He felt a little shy as he offered to take them for a ride, Pearl first, since she was the littlest.

His mother and Mr. Parker stood by the front gate watching the short trip. As he came back up, Thomas thought his mother looked young and happy, and Mr. Parker actually smiled when he lifted Pearl out of the wagon.

Indigo didn't need lifting. She clambered up, ready to go. Coon Dog stirred himself and came over to sit at Thomas's feet.

"Good boy, old Coon Dog, you," Thomas said, leaning over to pat him. "You want to have a turn, too? How about us going over to Hal's?"

"It's beginning to get dark," Thomas's mother cautioned.

"We'll be back 'fore dark," Thomas said and began leading the little pony along. "And if the pony gets tired, Indigo can walk back."

Both his mother and Mr. Parker laughed.

Thomas walked happily alongside the plodding little pony, leading her gently by the rein. Coon Dog walked at his heels, every now and then giving him a little nip. "Watch out, now, you old dog, you needn't get jealous," Thomas said.

Indigo got up on her knees in front of the wagon. "What are you going to name her?"

Thomas had been thinking about it. "Sally," he said after a moment, "That's a soft-sounding name, and she's got such soft brown eyes."

"Why don't you call her Woody? Because of all the wood you chopped this summer?"

"You shut up about that wood," Thomas said, but he wasn't really angry. Nothing could make him angry tonight.

"Sally. . . . Do you like Sally?" he asked the pony, who just kept stepping along.

"No, she likes Woody," Indigo said. "She looks soft, but she's got strength. Look how she pulls through this sand."

Thomas looked at Indigo in exasperation. "If you don't hush, you can just get out of the wagon. She's my horse, and I'll name her what I please." He walked a little farther, then looked back. "And I please to name her Woody. It suits her."

Indigo nodded and settled back again. "You're a good namer, Thomas," she said.

Hal was impressed with the pony, and a little jealous, too. At least Thomas thought so. "You can have a ride right now," he said to his friend. "Get out, Indigo, It's Hal's turn."

"You don't have to be so rude," Indigo said, climbing out of the wagon.

"Well, please get out. Thank you."

"But I don't want to ride in the wagon," Hal said. "I'd feel like a baby. How about unhitching her and letting me really ride her?"

Thomas shook his head. "Mr. Parker says she's only been trained to pull a wagon. He said I would have to ease into riding her."

"Well, let's ease into it now. She's so little if you don't start riding her right off, you're going to outgrow her 'fore you have much chance."

Thomas looked at him doubtfully. It might be too much for Woody all in the same day, just like Mr. Parker had said.

"Oh, come on, Thomas," Hal teased. "Why have a pony if you only use her to deliver groceries? What's the fun in that?"

"Your mother said we were to be home before dark," Indigo cautioned. "It's getting close to that now."

Thomas was thinking the same thing, but he didn't like Indigo reminding him. "Maybe we can take off the harness and walk her a little. Then I could just sit up on her back, not ride her, just give her the idea of it."

Indigo began shaking her head and that did it. Thomas started unbuckling the harness. When it was all free of the pony's body, he lapped it back over the wagon.

Woody stood quietly in her place. Thomas wished he

had a handful of hay or a piece of sugar to give her.

"Go on, Thomas, get up," Hal said.

"How can I get up? I've got nothing to step on."

"Here, I'll make you a mount." Hal leaned over and cupped his hands.

Thomas put one bare foot in Hal's hands and one hand over Woody's back, then gave a half jump to throw himself up over her back. Instead, he knocked Hal off balance, crashed into the pony's side, and slid to the ground. Rolling over in the sand, he was horrified to see Woody galloping away down the road.

"Woody, Woody," he cried, scrambling to his feet. "Hal! You dumbbell. Now see what you've done!"

"Dumbbell yourself! Don't you know how to get on a horse?"

"Don't yell, don't yell," Indigo pleaded, holding her hands to the sides of her face. "The poor little thing is already scared half to death."

She was right. Without another word Thomas motioned to Hal, and the two of them started running down the road after Woody.

It was pitch dark by the time Thomas got back to the barn with Woody. Lucky for him the pony had stayed on the road and not run off into the woods. She had trotted about a mile and then had stopped to graze in the long grass at the side of the road.

Thomas fastened the bolt across the barn door and leaned against it for a moment, dreading to go into the house.

There was a light in the kitchen as well as in the

sitting room. Thomas chose the kitchen and was sorry for the choice. Mr. Parker was sitting there at the table with a glass of buttermilk and a cold piece of cornbread. His gold watch was lying on the table.

He looked at Thomas with an unreadable expression on his face. It wasn't anger or frustration, but it certainly wasn't happiness.

"I guess Indigo told you."

Mr. Parker nodded.

"The pony's fine. It took me awhile to catch up with her and to get her home, but she's fine. Hal took the wagon to the store for me."

Mr. Parker stared at him a long time, and just when Thomas thought he couldn't stand the stare any longer, Mr. Parker spoke. "I don't know what to do about this, Thomas. I told you clearly not to try riding the horse just now."

Thomas felt a sick fear rise in him. Was Mr. Parker going to take Woody away from him? It was a thought that had haunted him from the minute he had seen Woody running down the road.

"She could have run into the woods and gotten lost, or snake bit. She could have broken a leg in a sinkhole."

Thomas could only nod his head. "Yes, sir, I know, and I'm awful sorry. I should have listened to you."

Mr. Parker picked up his watch and looked at it, shaking his head. Then he looked up at Thomas. "Well, I guess it wasn't such a terrible thing you did, really. It was only natural for you to want to try to ride your pony. Indigo said you truly wanted to ride her."

Thomas gulped. "Yes, sir. I really did. But I should have waited, tried her out in the pen in the back."

"That would have been wiser. A lot closer to obedience, too, I'd say." He picked up his cornbread. "You go on out to the pump and wash up some and then get on to bed. I'll finish eating this up. Waste not, want not, I always say."

"Yes, sir! That's a good saying," Thomas answered and fled to the porch. He stopped at the pump, put his arms around the post next to it, and hugged it close. "Oh, thank you, God. Thank you. I still got my pony."

SEVENTEEN
TOO CLOSE FOR COMFORT

While he was at the pump washing up, Thomas decided to check the barn door one more time. He didn't want anything or anybody bothering his beautiful little horse tonight.

Outside Coon Dog was sniffing about and whining a little as if he were uneasy about something. Thomas caught him around the neck and gave him a good scratching behind his ears and under his chin. "Don't be jealous, you old hound dog, you. You've got to help me look out for Woody, you know."

The barn door was bolted securely, so Thomas started back to the house. Coon Dog followed him back to the porch steps, but stopped there, sniffing the ground and looking at Thomas with a nervous little whine.

"Now stop that, Coon Dog. Don't get me scared,"

Thomas fussed and went on up into the dark loft.

His excitement and the heat kept Thomas awake for a long time. He was just beginning to relax when Coon Dog started growling. It was a warning growl, pitched low from deep in his throat.

Thomas came wide awake and sat upright. Coon Dog was quiet now, but the cookhouse seemed filled with other noises—scrapings and creakings and whispery sounds. He shivered in spite of the heat. Had the ghost come back again?

Then Coon Dog began barking excitedly, running across the yard. Thomas heard a heavy crash against the house. Coon Dog barked furiously. Then the sound of his yelps moved away from the house, as if he were chasing something or somebody.

Thomas hugged his arms tight around his body. Did dogs chase ghosts? Or if it was somebody, then who?

Thomas caught his breath. Maybe he'd rather have a ghost than Guillermo!

In a few minutes a hard rain began to fall, drumming on the tin roof close to Thomas's head like steady thunder. It wiped out all other sounds.

Thomas eased back onto his pillow and willed himself to go to sleep.

The following morning Thomas was awake and down in the yard before Lucy even came to start breakfast. Coon Dog came to meet him, jerking his tail and dripping all over Thomas's hands in an uneasy doggy greeting.

"Now, what was going on last night, you Coon Dog, you?"

Coon Dog panted eagerly as if he wanted to tell Thomas exactly what had gone on, if he just could.

Thomas pushed him away. "All right, now, let's go see how Woody is this morning. She probably didn't sleep much with all the ruckus in the yard."

Coon Dog followed him happily to the barn. Woody was standing in her stall, looking hopefully into her feed box. She glanced up at Thomas, and he didn't know if she felt afraid of him or disappointed in him or anything bad like that.

He went up to her and began gently patting her and rubbing her shoulders and back. "It's all right now, little girl. I'm not going to try to ride you right away. Right now I'm getting you some fresh hay. Mr. Parker had a whole bale delivered here." He paused for a moment filled with new wonder at Mr. Parker's generosity. "And I didn't even suspect anything about it."

"I knew about it!" Pearl said from the barn door. "Me and Indigo knew all about it. Papa said you had worked hard once you set your mind to it, and never asked off or run off either. He was going to reward you with something you needed and wanted."

Thomas didn't much like her intruding on his morning visit with his pony or her knowing about his personal affairs. Still, she had said something pretty nice. "Well, it was the best surprise of my life," he admitted.

She edged closer. "Are you going to take us for another ride this evening after work?"

This made Thomas cross again. "It's my pony. I've got to have a little time to get to know her. Don't be pestering me about rides all the time."

"That's selfish, Thomas."

"It's not either. Besides, girls don't need to be fooling around with ponies. She might kick you or even bite you."

Pearl shook her head. "Not Woody. Woody wouldn't."

Thomas finished filling the feed box. When he turned around, Pearl was still there.

"Why don't you go tell Indigo? She's calling you."

Pearl stuck out a trembling lower lip. "You're a mean boy. You don't deserve a sweet pony like Woody." With that she turned around and left, her little black boots stamping hard through the soft gray sand.

When Thomas had finished his visit with Woody, he went over to examine the ground around the cookhouse. He hoped to find some sign of whatever had been fooling around the house last night. There wasn't any. The hard rain had washed over the sand, smoothing over any footprints that might have been there.

Hearing someone at the gate, he wheeled around. Lucy was unlatching it to come in. If Coon Dog had been chasing a live man like Guillermo, that man certainly wouldn't have stopped to lock the gate after himself. It couldn't have been a man.

He spoke to Lucy with a certain amount of relief. "You're right about the ghost, you know."

"Which ghost is that?" she asked, hitching up her long skirt to go up the porch steps.

"The cookhouse ghost. You've been right all along."

Now he had her full attention. "Say what?" she demanded.

He explained about all the scary sounds he'd heard

in the night when he first started sleeping in the loft—
about the rattlesnake's warning, the icy hand, and now
something getting after Coon Dog. Something that
didn't need to lock or unlock a gate.

"Lawd, Lawd, Lawd," she wailed. "Whyn't you tell
me before? I wouldn't never allowed you to stay out
here."

Thomas shrugged. "Oh, he doesn't scare me all that
bad, Lucy, but I don't get much sleep. If he's come
back to stay, I'd just as soon move back into the
house."

Mr. Parker appeared in the kitchen door. He was all
dressed for work and probably had planned to ask
Lucy why she didn't have breakfast started. "What's
going on?" he asked instead.

"Something spooked the dog last night, Mr. Parker,
and spooked Thomas, too. He ain't big enough to be
sleeping out here all alone."

"No?" Mr. Parker said. "Why by Thomas's own accounts he's slept all over town, on the beaches, and in
the woods. The loft shouldn't be any threat to him."

Lucy stood her ground. "Mr. Parker, there's something just not right about this here cookhouse at night.
Tell him, Thomas. Tell him all about it."

It was the last thing Thomas wanted to do, but his
mother had come in and she was nodding that she
wanted to hear, too. He reluctantly repeated what he'd
told Lucy.

When he finished, his mother laughed nervously.
Her laughter hurt Thomas's feelings.

She put her arm around him and drew him to her.

"But Thomas, honey, we've lived here all these years and nothing like this has ever happened."

"Ain't nobody slept out here before," Lucy said. "You don't know what goes on less you be out here."

"Oh, for goodness sake," Mr. Parker said. He shook his head. "Well, there's one way to settle this. Tonight, I'll sleep in the loft. If there's a ghost out here and he spooks me, I'll admit it. There's not, of course, but we might as well get this settled before it gets out of hand."

The next morning at breakfast Mr. Parker appeared at the table out on the porch, fully dressed as usual but looking a little worn.

Thomas took his place, and the family said the blessing together. Mr. Parker ate awhile and then looked sharply at Thomas, who was too excited to eat, eager to know what had happened during the night.

Mr. Parker put down his napkin. "Well, Thomas, I didn't hear your ghost last night. The dog didn't bark. There were no rattlesnake rattles. I'm sorry to disappoint you and Lucy, but this is just an ordinary cookhouse with an ordinary, sturdy sleeping loft."

"Don't you think you ought to try it another night or so?" Thomas asked.

"I surely don't. I don't think that's necessary at all. I will say one thing. It is too hot to sleep up there in the summer. I rested very poorly. I'll try to make a trade with one of the local carpenters to put in dormer windows. In the meantime, you may come back into the house to sleep if you like."

"In my old room?"

His mother spoke up. "Well, dear, the girls are nicely settled there now, and later you'll want to go back to the loft. Why don't you continue sleeping on the divan in the sitting room? You get a lovely cross breeze there."

She smiled encouragingly at him, then buttered a hot biscuit and laid it on his plate. "Finish your breakfast now. And please, dear, let's just try to forget all this business about ghosts and rattlesnakes. It's upsetting the girls."

"Not me!" Indigo cried. "I don't want to forget it. I think it's exciting. And I'd like to hold the accursed fan myself one day."

"Indigo, what language!" Mr. Parker said.

Indigo blushed a little. "I mean the fan with the curse on it. Pearl's scared of it, you know."

Pearl nodded, her round face full of concern. "I am. I certainly am. Thomas. . . ."

Thomas interrupted in a hurry. "I'm going to try to forget it, if you say so." He knew he couldn't, but he wanted to get off the subject with Pearl's big mouth ready to spout.

Mr. Parker laid down his knife with a clatter. "Now, let's slow this conversation down a little. What fan? Why did you say it had a curse on it, Indigo? What kind of foolish talk is that?"

Now Indigo got really red. "The, uh, Aunt Lena's, uh, fan. The one with the dragons on it. I was just remembering something I heard once about Aunt Lena's fan."

Pearl's eyes glittered as she nodded her head at her father. "Yes! Thomas told us. . . ."

This time Thomas's mother interrupted Pearl. Looking at Thomas with an I'll-talk-to-you-later look, she said, "Dear little Pearl, there are all kinds of tales floating around Sarasota, and Thomas knows and loves every one of them. That doesn't make them true."

"You mean the fan really doesn't have a curse on it?" Indigo sounded disappointed.

"Well, I've never heard any such tale as that about the fan. It's all nonsense, of course. Do you think Aunt Lena would carry such a fan around with her? Even take it to church?"

Both girls shook their heads no, and Thomas excused himself from the table, angry at the whole tone of the conversation. His aunt would so carry such a fan. She'd even take a delight in it.

He stood behind the bench and looked at all of them defiantly. "Anyway, the story about the treasure under the house is true. My grandfather told me and he wasn't a liar!"

That night after the family had gone to bed, Thomas shut the door of the sitting room and latched it. Then he settled down on the divan to go to sleep. As his mother had predicted, there was a nice breeze cutting between the windows on opposite sides of the room. It blew against the mosquito netting draped over the divan. He ought to rest pretty comfortably in here once he got used to the idea.

When Coon Dog first began to growl, Thomas was so nearly asleep he thought he was dreaming about what had happened the night before last. Snuggling into his pillow, he only half heard Coon Dog begin to bark sharply. Then there was a quick, dull thud, and the barking stopped. Thomas opened his eyes wide.

Everything was perfectly still now. Had he dreamed the barking and the thump? Maybe he'd just heard a branch falling. Something simple like that.

Thomas thought of how Lucy was always saying she knew something in her bones. He knew in his bones he had heard real barking and a real thump. No dreams and no ghost either.

Somebody had hit poor Coon Dog to shut him up.

Guillermo. It had to be Guillermo. There just wasn't anybody else who would fool around their house at night.

Thomas eased up to sit on the side of the divan. Why hadn't Mr. Parker heard it? He was the head of the house now. Why didn't he just head on down here right now to help?

Now there was a new noise. A soft bumping and thumping somewhere under the house. Thomas felt the sweat break out on his face and run down his neck. There was a scraping and then a heavy falling sound, scraping and falling.

Someone's digging under the house! Thomas thought, wondering about the treasure he was sure lay buried there. Thomas got to his feet. If Mr. Parker wouldn't wake up now by himself, he'd go wake him. He would prove to him that something was going on right under their own cookhouse.

He eased up to his feet. Walking as lightly as he

could across the floor, he winced at every creak, stopped to listen, and then tiptoed on. The digging had not stopped.

He crept up the stairs and with just a moment's hesitation tiptoed into his mother's bedroom. His mother and Mr. Parker were both sound asleep under their mosquito net, Mr. Parker snoring softly.

Thomas went to his mother's side of the bed and shook her arm. She came suddenly awake with a gasp. Upon seeing Thomas, she sat up, clutching the sheet around her. "Thomas, what is it? Are you ill?"

"Shhh. Shhh. There's someone under the house."

"Oh, Thomas."

"There is. I'm sure there is."

Mr. Parker woke up with a snort. "What is it, dear?" Then he recognized Thomas's form in the darkness. "What in this world are you doing here?"

"Shhh. Shhh." Thomas's mother said. "Thomas says there's somebody under the house."

"There is," Thomas whispered. "He's digging under the cookhouse, I think. And he hit Coon Dog, too."

Mr. Parker jerked open the mosquito netting angrily and sat up, reaching for the kerosene lamp.

"Don't make a light," Thomas whispered anxiously. "You'll scare him away."

"Well, I certainly hope so."

The girls came running in. "What is it? What is it?"

"That does it," Mr. Parker said out loud, reaching for his trousers, which he quickly slipped into. He then lit the lamp and motioned with his head to Thomas. "All right, young man. You've got the whole house up.

Let's go find your ghost—or pirate—or maybe the devil himself for all I know."

"Papaaaa," wailed Pearl.

"Can I go?" Indigo begged.

"Certainly not. You girls go on back to bed. This is just more of Thomas's wild imaginings."

Thomas's mother got up. "Come, dears. I'll take you back to bed and stay until the house is all settled down again."

Thomas and Mr. Parker started down the steps. Mr. Parker pretended he wasn't afraid, but Thomas noticed that he held the lamp high and looked in every corner, stopping to listen every few steps.

Thomas thought once he heard a stumbling sound under the house, but Mr. Parker didn't seem to hear it. They went through the hall, peered into the parlor, the sitting room, and the dining room, and then went out onto the porch.

The lamp threw a beam of light across the yard out toward the shed where Coon Dog slept. Thomas saw Coon Dog rouse halfway to his feet and heard him whine.

"Let me go see about him and Woody, too, while you've got the light."

Mr. Parker sighed. "Thomas, you can see Coon Dog is all right. Whoever or whatever you thought you heard hasn't hurt him."

Thomas started to protest but decided it wouldn't do any good. Coon Dog was on his feet now and began loping toward them. Thomas had to admit to himself he looked the way he always did.

▲177

"Go back to the shed, boy," Mr. Parker said to Coon Dog. He motioned to Thomas with the lamp. "Come on now, Thomas, and let's get back to bed. I don't want to hear any more about this tonight, and preferably never. You did promise to forget it, you know. Why don't you try a little harder to do that?"

Thomas didn't know what to say. He didn't really want Mr. Parker to be angry with him. After all, he had gotten him the little horse. Still, it wasn't honest to pretend he didn't believe he'd heard the noises under the house.

"All right, sir," he said after a moment. "I'll try to forget about it." It seemed to be the only thing to say.

Thomas waited uneasily on the divan, listening to Mr. Parker's feet creak across the floor upstairs. There were soft murmurs from his mother, the girls, and Mr. Parker, and then silence.

Forget it? How could he forget what he knew he'd heard?

Thomas glanced over his shoulder at the open window behind him. A soft breeze was moving in, stirring the curtains. What else might move in?

Thomas cautiously leaned out the window, pulled the shutters closed, and latched them. He hurried across the room to do the same thing. He might feel hot, but at least whatever or whoever it was under the house couldn't come in on him without a racket.

He lay back on the divan, a lot of different feelings tumbling through his head. He was frustrated—Mr. Parker hadn't even looked under the house! He was scared—when had he ever locked the shutters against the night? And he was disgusted with himself for being scared.

It was the Parkers. Life had been simple before they'd moved in. In the good old days he and Hal would have been under the house and had the whole mystery solved in nothing flat.

Of course, Indigo might have gone with him if Mr. Parker hadn't interfered. Indigo was the only one of the Parkers who had the right ideas about a thing like this.

When that thought crossed his mind, Thomas blinked his eyes in surprise. Was there really something about Indigo that was good?

"Humph," he said out loud, sounding like Lucy. And then, like his mother, he thought, *That's a lot of nonsense.*

After that he concentrated on going to sleep.

The first thing Thomas did when he got up the next morning was to go out in the yard to check on Coon Dog.

He seemed fine enough, trotting across the yard to Thomas from out in the oak grove. He leaned against Thomas's leg and put his wet nose in his outstretched hand.

Thomas reached to pat him with the other hand and then rubbed his head. Under his fingers was a place that felt like a whole batch of ticks stuck together in a long line.

Coon Dog pulled back from the touch. Thomas bent over quickly. Taking Coon Dog's head between his hands, he saw a raised welt with dried blood crusted along one side.

"You did get hit! Poor old thing, you did get hit."

He let go of Coon Dog then and ran toward the house, almost colliding with Indigo. "He did get hit! Somebody was here and hit Coon Dog in the head. I heard it. I knew I heard it."

Indigo ran for her father, and Mr. Parker came out into the yard reluctantly, still drying his face from where he'd been washing up at the porch pump.

Thomas held Coon Dog while Mr. Parker looked. "Hmmm," he said, standing up again. "He's had a blow all right. Maybe he ran into something or a branch fell off the old oak by the shed."

Indigo and Thomas both looked at him, shaking their heads, not willing to believe that.

Mr. Parker gave a final wipe at his chin. "It does look like a direct blow. Maybe somebody hit him in the head with a chunk of wood."

At that moment Thomas ran for the cookhouse with Indigo right behind him. He dropped to his knees and started crawling under it. Indigo followed. Coon Dog came close behind, barking his head off.

Thomas got halfway under and then stopped, sitting back on his haunches. Right there in front of him were mounds of soft dirt and a gaping hole.

E I G H T E E N

GETTING DOWN TO BUSINESS

Thomas came out from under the house in a hurry. "I'm going for a shovel!" he cried, ready to start digging that very minute. He was sure that under these circumstances Mr. Parker wouldn't object. He was wrong.

Mr. Parker caught him by the arm. "Hold on there. This isn't a holiday, you know. We have to eat breakfast and go to work."

Thomas stared at him in amazement. He'd never felt less like going to the store. The most exciting thing in his whole life was trying to happen, and Mr. Parker wanted him to go out and deliver groceries.

"You don't even know there's anything to dig for," Mr. Parker said. "That hole under the house could be from the old days when people, including you, used to look for the treasure."

"But—but it's fresh dirt. You can see it's fresh dirt."

"Maybe Hal or even Sample was playing a trick on you," his mother said. Thomas looked at her, shaking his head. In a moment she was shaking her head, too. "The boys wouldn't have hit poor Coon Dog."

Finally Mr. Parker admitted that somebody must have been under the house the night before. "But who could it be?" he asked.

Thomas was certain he knew. "There was this sailor at Billy's fish camp," he blurted out. He hesitated a minute. He'd never told anybody but Hal about his experiences on the island. Mr. Parker probably wasn't going to believe him now, but he went on anyway.

"He was a big, wild-looking man named Guillermo. Wild and mean. Billy said he had some kind of treasure buried in Sarasota, and he was coming back to find it. I'm thinking the treasure may be the gold pieces in the box under our house."

Mr. Parker looked scornfully at Thomas. "That is a far-fetched idea."

Indigo, looking very excited, piped up. "But, Papa, maybe it isn't far fetched. The old man who claimed to have buried the treasure had a friend with him a couple of times. Why couldn't it be Gui—Gui— the wild man on the key?"

"Guillermo!" Thomas burst out. "He had been in jail for years when I saw him on the key. This is the first chance he's had to come back for the gold."

"It's been a long time since you saw this person,

Thomas. He's probably back in Cuba. And in jail again, hopefully."

"No, he's not. He's here. I saw him the night the train came in."

"Oh, mercy me," Thomas's mother said. "We'd better tell the marshal."

Mr. Parker looked at her unhappily. "The marshal will think we've gone daft."

"No, he won't," Thomas's mother said. "He's lived in these parts for years. He knows all the strange things that have happened."

Mr. Parker hesitated only a moment then. "I'll speak to him today. He and I probably ought to stand guard tonight, just in case the intruder comes back."

Lucy, who had been listening in the kitchen door, now moved to the table on the porch, carrying heavy bowls of grits and eggs. "No need to speak to the marshal. He can't do nothing about ghosts."

"Lucy! Ghosts don't dig holes!" Thomas's mother exclaimed.

Lucy put the bowls down. "How do you know? Do it say in the Bible ghosts don't dig holes?"

"That's enough about ghosts and about this whole conversation," Mr. Parker said. "Sit down and eat, Thomas. We've wasted enough time."

"All right, sir, but after work today I'm going to get Hal and we're going to tear up the ground under this house!"

"I'm going to dig this morning right after my chores," Indigo declared. "And Pearl, too."

"Not me," Pearl said and moved over to stand close

to Thomas's mother. His mother put an arm around her.

Thomas glared at Indigo. He couldn't stand the thought of her getting at the treasure dig first.

"Stay out from under the house, Indigo," Mr. Parker said. "There may be snakes." So, Mr. Parker had come to the rescue. Thomas didn't think he'd done it on purpose, but he was grateful anyway.

"Yes," Thomas said. "Snakes."

Indigo's face fell, and her father added, "This afternoon when Thomas gets through at the store, he can take Coon Dog and look things over first. Then you can go under with him and dig until dark."

He looked at Thomas's mother as if he felt he ought to explain why he'd given them permission to dig. "There's not going to be any peace around here until they get it out of their systems!"

She nodded, smiling. "And it's fun for them. After all, there's nothing wrong with children having fun." She looked down at Pearl. "Honey, you and I can put Woody away for Thomas tonight to save him time. Then we can sit on the steps and keep up with the digging. Until dark. Only until dark!"

"That's right," Mr. Parker said. "After that the marshal and I will stand guard." He sighed. "I wonder if I'm ever going to get a whole night's sleep again?"

"Sure you will," Thomas piped up. "Me and Hal will stand guard with you and the marshal, and we'll catch that Guillermo for sure!"

Mr. Parker frowned. "No, I don't think that's a good idea. That is a job for men."

"It certainly is," his mother said, and that was the end of that.

Late that afternoon when Hal and Thomas dropped to their knees and started to crawl under the house, Coon Dog growled a protest. "Come on, dog," Thomas said. Coon Dog followed, but still made threatening sounds from deep in his throat.

"Is it all right under there? Can I come now?" Indigo whispered fiercely from the edge of the house.

"Why are you whispering?" Thomas whispered back. "Neither the ghost nor Guillermo's going to get after you until dark."

"Does she have to come under here with us?" Hal demanded.

Thomas didn't look at him, but kept crawling. "Yes, I guess so."

"But we never had no girl work with us before!"

"She ain't a girl . . . a girl girl, you know. She's Indigo."

"They're all the same to me, and I don't think she has a right to be butting into our business."

Thomas sat down in the sand and turned to look at Indigo. She was watching him with an expression that said she halfway expected him to tell her to go away.

He looked at Hal and then started crawling again. "Well, it's kind of her house now, too," he said.

Hal got red in the face. "If you're choosing her over me, Thomas, I'm leaving!"

Thomas shrugged. "Suit yourself."

Hal crawled out from under the house and made an ugly face at Indigo as he passed.

Indigo dropped to her knees and crawled under the house to where Thomas was sitting. "I'm sorry I caused you a fight with Hal."

Thomas waved one dirty hand. "Oh, that wasn't no fight. Hal's just got to go off and cool his red hair down. He'll be back."

Indigo nodded and looked around. "Where shall we dig?"

They had already passed the hole at the edge of the house, and Thomas pointed to another pile of dirt and a new hole. The sand on the surface was dry, but a few inches underneath it seemed moist. It wasn't a new digging, but it wasn't a real old one either. "He's been here at least one other night," he said wonderingly, "and we didn't even hear him."

He scrunched his shoulders together and looked at Indigo. "Don't it give you the creeps to think he was here, and we didn't even know it? We could've been murdered in our beds—our throats slit from ear to ear."

Indigo's eyes flashed. "You hush. You can't scare me off, you know. Now let's get to digging before he comes back."

She had a hoe and Thomas a short-handled spade. It was awkward working under the house. Thomas wondered how in the world Guillermo had done it. Thomas wished the house had been built up really high, like some of those old pioneer shacks down by the bay.

And Coon Dog didn't help either, digging with his front paws and throwing sand all over them. Finally Thomas ran him off.

They dug at random and not very deep. The farther under they went, the darker it got.

"Let's dig together to save time," Thomas said. "Let's try over by the stump of that tree. Probably no one ever dug there."

She nodded and crawled with him to the stump.

"Don't go too far," Thomas's mother cautioned from the steps. "It's getting late, and you're going to have to bathe before supper."

Thomas heard Mr. Parker speaking to someone in the street in front of the house. He knew that once Mr. Parker got home, their digging time really would be short. "Hurry," he said to Indigo. "Dig fast."

"I'm digging," she said crossly. "It's harder with the hoe—there are still roots here!" She chopped at the dirt, pulling the sand away as she went. Thomas spaded just at the other side of where she was working.

Suddenly they both heard the hoe click against something hard. They stopped, staring at each other.

"It's probably a shell," Indigo said, but in half a second she was hoeing away at the soft sand.

"Move over," Thomas said, shoving her aside. He began to dig hard where they had heard the sound. There was nothing.

"You missed it," Indigo said crossly. "It was right near the top, and you've probably covered it over now."

"Dig." Thomas said. He dropped the spade and with his bare hands began going through the sand he had shoveled aside. And then he felt it. Something hard, and not a seashell.

In a second he had it out of the sand. It was a small oblong box about a foot long, dark in color and uneven under his fingers with some kind of carving.

"Is it the red-lacquered box?" Indigo cried, bending over his shoulder.

"It may be—I think it is! At least the bottom part of it!"

The box had no lid and was full of sand. He carefully raked the sand out of the box, emptying it completely.

Then he sank back on his haunches, sick with disappointment. There was nothing in the box, no gold, no treasure of any kind. "It's just plain empty," he said, hefting it in his hand. "Not even a lid."

Indigo touched his arm. "But, Thomas, don't you see? That means the gold could have fallen out. The lid could be right here somewhere and the gold, too!"

She began combing through the sand with her fingers. Thomas got down on his hands and knees and dug furiously beside her.

"Indigo, Thomas! Come out with you now," Mr. Parker called. "It's too dark to dig anymore, and your supper's ready."

Thomas and Indigo looked at each other. It was pretty dark. They had scarcely noticed.

"We'll come back tomorrow and find it," Indigo said.

"If Guillermo doesn't find it first," Thomas wailed.

At the porch pump Thomas washed the box off before he sat down to supper and went to place it on the buffet in the dining room. The whole time he was eating he kept looking at it. So did the rest of the family. Even Mr. Parker.

It was a beautiful little thing, or had been. There were dragons carved all around just as on the fan, and it was lacquered over in deep red. Parts of the paint had chipped away, exposing a rich dark wood.

Mr. Parker thought it was teakwood.

"But the gold?" Thomas burst out suddenly. "It's more important than the box, and it's still there. I just know it!"

Mr. Parker leaned forward, actually looking a little excited. "Tomorrow you should take the rake and go through all the sand in that area—thoroughly." He threw up his hands. "What am I saying? You children have bewitched me."

Thomas's mother shook her head at him, laughing. "You're not bewitched. The children found the box, and Aunt Lena already had the fan. Why shouldn't we believe the rest of the story is true as well?" She paused. "Of course, since the box was empty, we have to face the possibility that someone found the gold long ago."

Thomas shook his head. "Guillermo doesn't think so."

Mr. Parker groaned. "Oh, Thomas. You and your Guillermo. It's hard for me to know what is real and what is fancy."

Thomas excused himself from the table. He went over to the buffet and picked up the red box. "My box is real. And the gold, too. And it's still under there. I just know it."

Indigo jumped up. "Your box? But I found it. It should be mine."

Thomas held it against his chest. "You only touched it with the hoe. I found it with my bare hands."

Mr. Parker had gotten up. "Now, Thomas, I wouldn't think a boy would want a fancy thing like that, and Indigo did find it first."

Thomas held the box tightly. Surely, surely Mr. Parker wouldn't make him give it to Indigo. His mother was shoving back her chair to get up, but Mr. Parker put a hand on her shoulder. "One moment, dear."

He looked as if he were trying to make up his mind about something. "The point is, Thomas does want it. And as I study on the matter I can see why, and why it's his by rights. It was buried on his grandfather's land before the house was built. And before the Parkers even thought of coming to Sarasota." He looked over at Indigo, who was busy making a face at Thomas.

"Fair's fair, Indigo. Now let that be the end of it," he said.

Thomas didn't know what to say. He felt very strange having Mr. Parker take his side in this quarrel.

Fair is fair, he thought. *And Mr. Parker does say what he means and mean what he says.* Thomas went on and admitted something else to himself, since fair was fair. Mr. Parker, like Indigo, had some good things about him.

He looked over at his stepsister. He didn't want Indigo to be angry with him, and maybe hurt with her father as well. Hoping to change the atmosphere in the room, he said, "I'm going to sit up all night tonight.

If Guillermo comes back, he won't catch me sleeping."

"That won't be necessary," Mr. Parker said. "The marshal will be over soon, and we'll take care of the situation."

Thomas nodded, but he knew there was no way he was going to miss standing this watch. He already knew exactly where he was going to sit.

Later that evening the marshal came over, and he and Mr. Parker went outside. Thomas sat near the window in the dark sitting room. He was listening with all his might for some sound that would warn him Guillermo was coming for another try at the treasure.

He was also thinking about the ghost in the cookhouse. He hadn't seen him or heard him lately, but he had to exist. Guillermo had still been in jail in Cuba when Thomas first felt the icy hand on his ankle and heard the eerie sounds in the cookhouse. Guillermo couldn't have had anything to do with all that.

Not only did Lucy believe in the ghost, she didn't think it had gone away. "Poor soul can't leave or rest," she had told Thomas privately. "Can't rest because of that evil treasure."

Thomas hugged his arms around his knees in the darkness. If the treasure were evil, he wasn't sure he wanted to find it himself. Maybe he could take it to the preacher to pray over. The Holy Ghost was more powerful than any regular one.

A board creaked in the hall. Thomas stiffened, listened, and then slowly turned his head toward the door. Another creak—this time closer.

He held his knees tightly as the door opened and a

small figure stood there outlined in the dim light. It was Indigo.

"What are you doing here?" he whispered fiercely, irritated that he'd let her scare him.

She crept over toward where he was sitting. "I want to stand guard with you. Father is out front in the orange grove, and Marshal Vinson's out back in the oaks. I think the two of us ought to be right here over the treasure."

It made sense. Two were always better than one in a situation like this. And it might mean she wasn't holding a grudge about the box.

"Do you think we ought to go out on the porch where we could hear better?" she whispered.

He thought a minute. "No. If we go out there, old CD would come running, and that would warn Guillermo off."

She nodded and sat down in the wooden arm chair near him. "Thomas?"

He frowned and put his finger to his lips.

"Thomas, I want to tell you something."

He threw up his hands, exasperated. "Be quiet now. You can't stand watch and talk all the time."

"Well, never mind, you stupid boy. I only wanted to tell you it was all right about the box!" Sitting back in her chair, she didn't say anything else at all.

At the breakfast table the next morning Mr. Parker scratched his arms through his shirt sleeves and then the back of his neck. "With mosquitoes like we have, we don't need any other kind of villains," he said crossly.

Guillermo hadn't shown up last night, and Thomas thought Mr. Parker was as disappointed as the rest of them.

"I'm glad it was only mosquitoes that got after you," his mother said. "I was so uneasy I didn't sleep a wink last night."

"Me neither," Thomas said.

"Ha!" Mr. Parker said. "You were sleeping like the dead when I came in to wake you this morning." He looked over at Indigo. "And you, Miss Priss, hard floor and all, were snoring like a buzz saw." Indigo blushed furiously under her tanned skin. Mr. Parker took a large mouthful of grits dripping with butter. "I haven't made up my mind yet, but what I ought to give you a licking. The idea of your pulling a stunt like that!"

"Of course you won't give her a licking," Thomas's mother said. "She's much too big for that. Besides, she meant no harm at all in what she did."

Mr. Parker sighed. "But you won't ever do such a thing again now, Indigo, will you?"

"No, Papa," she said, looking at Thomas. "That is, not without asking."

"There'll be no reason to ask. The marshal and I agree that since you found the box empty, whoever was digging the other night, or at some other time, found the box and the gold. He's long since skedaddled by now."

Thomas shook his head. "But the box wasn't where

anyone had been digging, and if someone had found it, why wasn't it just lying on the ground?"

Mr. Parker shoved his chair back and got up from the table. "I don't know why. I have no idea why. I just want to get on with my normal life again. That's all I want. I've got work to do. These are hard times!"

Indigo got up and went over to her father. Then leaning against him, she put her arm around his waist. "I'm sorry if I did something to displease you, Papa."

He patted her head, and she continued softly. "And I want to ask you now, even if you're tired of this whole subject and don't want to hear any more about it, may Thomas and I keep digging? Just quietly, and without bothering you at all about any of it?"

He threw up his hands. "Dig. Dig. Just dig by daylight and only when your mother or Lucy is here to listen out for you."

"Who gonna listen out for me?" Lucy said.

N I N E T E E N

GUILLERMO!

Thomas put Woody in her stall and added hay to her feed box. Pearl stood inside the shed door and watched. She had taken over this chore for him since he, Indigo, and Hal had started digging under the house. It hadn't taken Hal any time at all to get over his anger.

Pearl seemed disappointed to be relieved of her job. "Never mind," Thomas said. "You'll get plenty more chances, but tonight I won't be digging. I'll be getting ready to go to church night."

She nodded and reached over to give Woody a little pat. "Good night, honey," she said. "Maybe Thomas will take me for a nice, long ride tomorrow afternoon."

"I might," Thomas said, busying himself at the feed box. When he looked around again, she had gone into the house.

Thomas rubbed Woody's back gently. "I'll share you a little," he whispered, "but don't forget you're my baby." He gave Woody a final pat. "Well, I've got to go on to the house. I've got to eat supper and take me a whole bath."

His mother and Mr. Parker took Sunday and the preparations for Sunday very seriously. He knew without asking that they wouldn't want him digging tonight. They'd want him to eat early supper so he could be ready to take his turn in the galvanized tub behind the cookstove.

Going up the porch steps, he realized he wasn't very disappointed in not working under the house tonight. Even with all the digging he and the others had done, all they'd found, besides the red-lacquered box, were some bleached-out seashells and a few shards of Indian pottery.

And Lucy needn't have worried. The ghost hadn't shown up again either.

Thomas was beginning to wonder if Mr. Parker wasn't right after all. Maybe Guillermo had found the gold and skedaddled—if it had really been Guillermo under the house.

After his bath, Thomas waited in the sitting room with his mother and the girls for Mr. Parker to come in and lead family devotions. They'd all had their baths except Mr. Parker. He had a summer cold and was afraid of taking a chill.

▲196

He finally came into the room holding a handkerchief to his nose and looking distracted. "I can't find my watch," he said. "I must have left it in the cash register at the store. I remember putting it there today before I scoured out the meat chest."

"My goodness, Albert, it isn't like you to forget anything, much less your watch," Thomas's mother said.

"It isn't like me at all. It's the cold I caught in the woods the other night." Frowning a little at Thomas, he sat down. "There wasn't enough cash in the drawer to bring home. Everybody charged or traded today. So I just locked the register and came home. I never thought about my watch."

Mr. Parker then picked up the big Bible from the table and opened it to the place marked with a piece of velvet. He began to read, hesitating from time to time as if he were having a hard time seeing in the dim light of the kerosene lamp.

Thomas wondered if it was the light or his cold or worrying over his watch that was causing him to do that. He knew for sure that Mr. Parker had cut the reading short.

Then Mr. Parker prayed, just as he always did. He remembered each member of the family by name, the church, the preacher, and two of his customers down with malaria. At the very end he told the Lord in a sort of apologetic way that he hoped his watch was safe in the cash register. Then he said a quick amen, and all the family said amen after him.

Mr. Parker blew his nose and looked at his wife. "I

think I'll run by the store and get it. I've carried that watch since I wasn't much older than Thomas here. My grandpa gave it to me, and his pa gave it to him. I set great store by it."

"Oh, you mustn't go out in the night air, dearest," Thomas's mother said. "You'll catch your death. If the watch is in the cash register, it's quite safe. Isn't it?"

Mr. Parker shook his head. "A few days ago I would have said yes. All this talk about treasure hunters and pirates and wild sailors has gotten me on edge."

He gave Thomas a glum look. Thomas got the strong feeling Mr. Parker thought he was at the bottom of every bit of his edginess.

And in a way he was. Thomas thought maybe he could make it up to him. "Why don't I go and get your watch for you? I can get there and back in a jiffy."

Mr. Parker looked a little doubtful, but after a moment he said, "Well, you have unlocked the store before. I guess you can do it tonight." Then he frowned and shook his head. "But you'd have to have light to get into the cash register."

"I could light the lamp."

Mr. Parker sighed and blew his nose into his big white handkerchief. "All right then, but take Coon Dog with you. We've never had any trouble with hooligans, but you never know anymore."

"I'm on my way," Thomas said, pleased to have an errand at the store that was partway grown-up for a change. He scooted out of the sitting room, called to Coon Dog, and was off in a flash.

It was dark down by the store. The street lamp over the well at Five Points didn't shed much light down this far, and there was only a quarter moon. Thomas was the only one around. There weren't even any cows sleeping in the street. It was kind of eerie. For once in his life Thomas was glad that God stayed awake all night keeping an eye on things.

At the store Thomas fingered the front lock, fitted the key in, and opened the door. The moon shone dimly through the front windows, and by its light he made his way to the main counter where the lamp was stored.

He took one of the sulphur-dipped sticks of wood out of the can and struck it against the stone knife sharpener. When it flared, he lit the wick of the lamp and adjusted it to keep it from burning too high and smoking up the store. Thomas stepped back, feeling in his pocket for the key to the cash register.

Coon Dog was at his heels. Suddenly he wheeled around, facing the door, and began growling deep in his throat in the same warning way Thomas had heard the last night he'd slept in the loft.

Thomas felt a chill run up the back of his neck, crinkling his scalp. He saw the shadow of a man move across the front of the store, and then in just a moment the shadow materialized in the doorway. Thomas gasped. It was Guillermo!

He was every bit as big as Thomas remembered. His black eyes glittered in the glow of the lamp, and his gold teeth flashed in a wide and evil grin. Eyeing

Coon Dog, he fingered the hilt of the knife stuck in his belt.

Thomas clamped one hand on Coon Dog's collar, half for the comfort of touching him, half to keep him from lunging at the sailor. That knife could do more damage than the chunk of wood had.

"You a smart boy," Guillermo said. He didn't move closer, but studied Thomas thoughtfully. "You be the niño from Señor Billy's camp. I see you around town. I watch you digging under your house last night." He looked around the store. "But you dig too late. This a fine new store. I think your papa built this store with my gold."

"No, no," Thomas cried. "My papa's dead, and he didn't find your gold. Neither did my stepfather. He won't even go under the house."

"He didn't get my gold, huh?" Guillermo rested one big thumb against his teeth. Then looking at the cash register, he grinned again. "But there's money there, no?"

Thomas held the cash register key tightly in his hand and shook his head furiously. "No, no money either. Mr. Parker hasn't got any money. I just came to get his. . . . " He stopped, horrified at what he'd almost said.

But even what he'd said was too much. Guillermo flashed his teeth again and slid his long knife out of his belt. Watching Coon Dog, he moved toward the counter and the cash register.

Coon Dog began to bark sharply, pulling hard against Thomas's grip. Trying to control him, Thomas caught at his collar with both hands and dropped the key to the cash register.

Guillermo heard the key clink. When he saw what it was, he laughed and reached over to pick it up. In that moment Coon Dog lunged hard against his collar, broke Thomas's hold, and clamped his teeth into Guillermo's leg.

Guillermo screamed in pain. He angrily grabbed Coon Dog's collar and raised his knife high to strike.

Thomas jumped for his arm and tried to wrap his own arms around it. Guillermo shook him like a rag doll and then with a mighty sweep sent him flying backward across the counter.

Thomas felt a shock of pain in his back at the same time he heard the crash of the oil lamp on the floor behind the counter. For a few seconds the store was quite dark. Coon Dog growled wildly and Guillermo cursed. Suddenly a smoky flame appeared from the other side of the counter.

The lamp must have fallen near the stack of old newspapers Mr. Parker kept for wrapping groceries. In a second the flame leaped high along a work apron hanging on the counter.

In this new light Thomas had an instant, terrible picture of the whole store awash with flames. With no fire truck in Sarasota, most buildings that caught fire burned to the ground.

Thomas flung himself again at Guillermo. "The store's going to catch on fire, you crazy man. You've got to help me!"

Guillermo gave a mighty push separating himself

from Thomas and Coon Dog. "Help you? You can burn in hell, you blasted niño!" He wheeled and ran out of the store, Coon Dog grabbing at his heels.

"Coon Dog!" Thomas cried once, then raced around the counter, fell on his knees, and began beating at the fire with his hands. The varnish on the cabinet behind the burning papers was beginning to blister. He knew that in a moment the cabinet would catch on fire.

O God, you've got to help me, he prayed. *Mr. Parker loves this store. He'll never get over losing it, and he'll never forgive me for burning it down.*

And it was going to burn down. Thomas leaped to his feet. He had to run away again! Like Guillermo. Really run away. And never come back.

He glanced at the cash register almost surrounded by flames now and suddenly thought of the watch. He could try to save that, even if he got burned trying. But he had dropped the key. *Where is it?* he wondered in near panic. Then he got down on his hands and knees and began crawling around on the floor. Suddenly he spotted the softly gleaming key near a wooden barrel and grabbed it.

Rushing back to the cash register, he was hardly conscious of the flames blazing so close. The metal of the register burned his finger as he was opening the drawer, but it didn't matter. He snatched the watch, which felt hot, and raced from the store.

On the street, Thomas tried to think how he could run away.

Could he go home and get Woody out of the barn

without being seen? Could he hide out in the woods without Woody and steal a ride on the next train leaving town?

Unable to think clearly, he just started running. He didn't even see the preacher until he'd crashed into him.

The preacher gasped and righted the both of them. "Well, Thomas, what's your hurry? You look like you're running from the devil or with him." He caught Thomas's arms and looked him in the face. "You're not running away again?"

Thomas gulped. But suddenly and surely he knew. He wasn't running away. He couldn't. Not even if Marshal Vinson put him in the jailhouse. "No, no," he cried. "The store's on fire! The store's on fire!"

The preacher gave him a shove. "Run tell your pa. I'll ring the church bell to sound the alarm!"

He and Thomas started running at the same time.

It seemed to Thomas that in no time at all Main Street was full of people. He saw his mother, Indigo, and Lucy join with other women and children in a line stretched from the well at Five Points to the burning store. Hal and Sample were drawing buckets of water from the well and passing them down the line to the men at the store.

There was a lot of shouting and running about. Dogs were barking, and at one point three frightened cows came charging around the corner and down Main Street, scattering the water brigade.

Thomas worked alongside the men at the store,

hauling boxes of canned goods and bolts of material out into the open. Mr. Parker seemed to be everywhere at once. He had fought the flames as long as there had been any point in doing so, and now he directed the attempts to save as much of the merchandise as possible.

On one of his trips outside, Thomas caught a glimpse of his Aunt Lena sitting in her small carriage, waving her arms and shouting orders that none of them could hear.

It seemed like hours, but Thomas knew it was only minutes when Marshal Vinson shouted, "Get out! Get out! Everybody out now!"

Thomas snatched at a bolt of handmade lace. He wasn't going to leave until Mr. Parker did.

"It's gotten to the attic," a man yelled. "Everybody out before somebody gets killed!"

Mr. Parker ran up to Thomas and caught him around the shoulders. "Come on now, boy!" he cried. "You've done enough."

Thomas groaned. He'd done enough all right. He had burned down Mr. Parker's store.

Thomas grabbed for a final load just as Mr. Parker did. In that instant a huge section of the ceiling crashed right behind them. They were knocked forward by a rush of blistering air and a shower of burning splinters and hot coals.

They both dropped what they were carrying and ran. At the door, men snatched at them, pulling them free from the roar of the flames. Thomas felt hands beating at his hair and across his shoulders and back, striking away the hot cinders and ashes.

"You like to got killed!" somebody cried, and somebody else agreed, "Darn near, darn near."

He broke away. "I'm all right. Just let me be."

Mr. Parker was coughing and gasping. Thomas saw the preacher put an arm around him and force him further from the store. "Come away now, Albert," he said. "Come away. It's all over."

Thomas moved through the crowd blindly, wanting only to get away from the grasping hands and anxious faces for a while. When he was free from them all, he crawled up under a spreading oak tree and collapsed on the ground.

He took a few deep, uneven breaths and for the first time allowed himself to look at his hands. He'd felt the pain in them while he was carrying the boxes out of the store. Somehow it made him feel better. He deserved to feel some pain.

He should have let Coon Dog jump Guillermo at the start. He should have grabbed a chair and gone after Guillermo himself. He and Coon Dog together could have run him off.

Where was Coon Dog now? Was he all right?

As silent as Indians, Hal and Indigo slipped under the low branches and dropped to the ground beside him.

Hal looked at him a moment, then said, "It's awful about the store. What are you going to do now?"

"I don't know," Thomas answered helplessly.

Hal put out his hand and touched Thomas's shoulder. "If you're thinking of leaving, I'll go with you. The two of us could make out fine."

"I'll go, too," Indigo said. "Three's better than two."

Thomas felt Hal stiffen beside him, ready to object, but then he settled back down without a word.

"No, but thank you. There's no need for either of you to go. A body ought not to ever run away unless he just has to go for some powerful good reason."

They all raised their heads, hearing the preacher calling in the distance. "Hal! Hal! Hal Watson, where are you?"

Thomas smiled in spite of his sadness. "I told you, Indigo. He never slumbers nor sleeps." He turned to Hal. "You better go right on now, 'fore he raises the town again."

Hal gave him a little push that was almost like a hug and crawled away and out from under the tree.

Thomas and Indigo leaned back against the tree, Thomas carefully because of some tender places. After a moment he said to her, "I burned my hands kind of bad. I can't see them, but I think they're bleeding. Something's wet and running."

"Oh, Thomas." She reached out to touch his hands and then drew back. "Do they hurt something terrible?"

"Yes."

She leaned against him. "You can cry if you feel like it. I swear I won't tell."

He believed her. "I don't want to cry." He didn't, not anymore.

She touched his arm. "We better get home now, Thomas. Mama can wash your hands and put aloe on them."

He groaned out loud. "How can I go home? I feel so bad about the store."

"I know. But let's go anyway."

T W E N T Y

PROMISES

Coon Dog met Thomas and Indigo at the gate. Hugging him, Thomas felt a deep gash on his shoulder and smelled a strong odor of turpentine. Somebody had cleaned up the ugly wound. "Poor old fella," Thomas murmured, rubbing his head.

Coon Dog followed them to the edge of the back porch, then sat down and watched them go up the steps.

Thomas and Indigo moved quietly to the kitchen door and peered into the lighted room. The family was all there, including his Aunt Lena, who was sitting in a kitchen chair, drinking a mug of coffee. Mr. Parker was pacing the floor, a wet dressing on his neck and shoulders.

Lucy was mumbling away at the stove, getting ready to put in a pan of biscuits. She was the first to spot them. "Do, Lawd! Here they is. Thank you, Jesus."

Thomas saw her heading over to grab him, but his mother beat her to it. She was crying a little, but then she stopped and directed him to the table. There she began to wash and dress his hands with aloe pulp and linen bandages, murmuring soothing little noises as she worked.

Looking nervously at Mr. Parker, Thomas began to tell what had happened at the store. Mr. Parker had already heard some of it, but he listened again without saying anything. Aunt Lena didn't do anything more than grunt at the telling, but she looked hard at Thomas and he figured she was biding her time before lighting into him.

"Guess what?" Pearl broke in, her eyes as bright as two stars in her dirty little face. "The marshal brought Coon Dog home and he said he was a hero. That old Guillermo came back to the fire, probably to steal something, and Coon Dog grabbed him and held on to him until some of the men could wrestle him down and put him in the jailhouse!"

Lucy banged a pan on the stove. "Trouble with that wild man ain't over. That little old jailhouse not going to hold him long."

Aunt Lena pushed up from her chair with a groan. "Well, this old lady is getting herself home while he's still safely locked up." Then she stared at Thomas, and he got ready for her attack.

She shook her head. "Thomas, you scalawag!" That sounded like a pretty good beginning. And then she shook her head again and added, "The Lord is good. I don't know as I could stand it to lose all the Tisdale men."

While Thomas stared at her in amazement, she said apologetically to Mr. Parker. "Or you either, of course, sir." With that she was out of the kitchen, and they heard her hallooing for Hooper to drive her home.

Lucy called them to the table then, but Thomas found he wasn't very hungry. The aloe had already cut down some of his pain, and he wished he could put some on the dread that was like a cramp in his chest. He'd been surprised and grateful for what his aunt had said, but Mr. Parker would be something else again.

Wanting to get past whatever was coming, he pushed back from the table and went to stand by his stepfather. "I'm sorry, Mr. Parker, sir, Pa. I'm just awful sorry about your store." He wanted to say that he felt sorry for Mr. Parker himself, but it didn't seem to be the right kind of thing for a boy to say to a grown man.

Mr. Parker looked at him for a moment as if he weren't even sure who Thomas was. Then he blinked his eyes and said, "I know you're sorry. We all are. I'm sorry I sent you down there in the first place. I shouldn't have when I was feeling so uneasy. Maybe if you hadn't been in the store, Guillermo would have gone on by."

"Maybe," Thomas murmured, still expecting Mr. Parker to accuse him of being the main one responsible for the fire.

Thomas's mother got up and went to stand by Mr. Parker. "It doesn't matter now what we should or shouldn't have done. That's all behind us. And Aunt Lena's right. The important thing is that you're safe and Thomas is safe."

Mr. Parker looked up at her in surprise and caught her hand. "Why, my dearest one, don't you think I know that? God knows how grateful I am. We could have been killed or hurt badly or some of our friends trying to help us. Nothing in the store nor the store itself was worth that." He got up from the table suddenly. "We'll have to rebuild it, of course. I don't know just how, but we will."

Mr. Parker looked at his wife, then at Thomas and shook his head. "You know, Thomas, the strangest thing flashed through my mind this evening when I saw the ceiling crashing down on us. I thought we were both going to die. And in that instant I wished I had told you that I'd always planned to get you a real horse someday."

Thomas's mouth dropped open. He'd been sure Mr. Parker would be so angry with him about the store that he might even run him off. Instead, Mr. Parker was acting like the fire wasn't really Thomas's fault and telling him that in that most dangerous moment he'd thought of him and. . . .

"A horse?" Thomas's voice trembled. "A real horse?"

Mr. Parker nodded, smiling a little bit for the first time tonight. "Yes. One primarily for work, of course, but also one to ride out in the country—when you have the time. I'm still going to get one for you. I'm afraid it won't be for a long time now. In these hard times it's not going to be easy to start over."

Thomas nodded. "Yes, sir. I understand. I can wait."

Indigo came up to her father and caught his arm. "And me, too, Papa? Will you get me a real horse? I can help work now, and I can wait a long time, too."

He covered her hand with his. "Well, daughter, I'll certainly do my best."

Indigo flashed Thomas a wide grin. He grinned back. Real horses to ride free as the wind way out into the country! "Then I can have Woody," Pearl burst out. "Can't I have Woody then, Thomas?"

Thomas gulped. "Well, maybe not *have*. I don't know as I'd ever give Woody away. She's too special. But you can ride her all you want, if you are very careful with her."

"She'll be careful," Mr. Parker said. "She'll be older then and wiser."

He reached for his watch and stopped, looking half sad and half embarrassed. "I forgot. I guess the one thing I'm going to miss is my watch."

Thomas jumped up like a startled frog, remembering the watch in his pocket for the first time since he'd run from the store. "I've got it! I've got it!" he cried. Then he reached into his pocket and got out the watch and handed it to Mr. Parker.

With a look of amazement, Mr. Parker took the watch, held it to his ear, and then opened it up. He looked at Thomas, then opened his mouth and shut it again, swallowing hard.

Thomas knew what he wanted to say and answered him. "You're very welcome."

Mr. Parker stared down at the watch again.

"Eleven-thirty! It's eleven-thirty and we're still up! That will never do. It's time this family got itself to bed. But first, we'll have our prayer time and thank God we're still a complete family and that we have health and strength to rebuild our store."

Thomas nodded. He didn't resent Mr. Parker calling them a family, and nobody had to tell him how much he had to thank God for.

"Thomas," Mr. Parker said, "move these chairs in a circle." He looked down then at Thomas's bandaged hands. "Well, maybe Indigo should do it tonight." Thomas was grinning and Mr. Parker added, "Don't think you'll escape work for long. As soon as your hands heal, I expect you on the job."

Thomas kept on grinning. It was good to have his stepfather acting like himself again. And he wanted to help rebuild the store.

"Yes, sir, Pa," he said.

After the rest of the family had gone to bed, Thomas sat on the divan, his head propped on one hand. He was too tired to sit up straight and too excited to go to sleep.

He tensed, hearing the floorboards creaking in the hall as someone moved stealthily along. Then there was the sound of the door opening slowly on its hinges.

Guillermo! Guillermo had broken out of jail just as Lucy had warned.

Then he relaxed. The footsteps had moved out of the house not in. He knew in his bones that it wasn't

Guillermo and it wasn't the ghost either. He eased off the divan and padded across the floor in the direction of the footsteps.

He found Indigo sitting on the back steps, resting against the balustrade. He dropped down beside her, and they exchanged a silent grin. Then he leaned close and whispered, "Ain't it a wonder about the horses, Indigo?"

She nodded eagerly, hugging her knees to her chest. "And he means it. He wouldn't have said it if he didn't mean it."

Now Thomas was quiet, savoring the thought of the promised horses like a special treasure. After a while he said, half joking, "If you stay out here, the ghost or Guillermo will get you."

Indigo inched closer to Thomas and sat staring a moment out over the big dark yard. "Guillermo, maybe," she said then, "but not the ghost. Thomas, I have to tell you something. You didn't really hear a ghost the night you thought you heard one."

He forgot to be quiet and said out loud, "What are you talking about? I certainly did. I felt the hand as sure as I'm sitting here, and I heard the rattler."

"Oh, Thomas, please don't be mad, but I did it. I dipped my hand in the bucket of ice left from the wedding and caught your foot when you were coming down the ladder. You'd been so mean. I wanted to pay you back."

He stared at her, not willing to believe she'd really done it.

"And I got the snake rattles from Sample. He gave

me a string of them from his collection. He didn't know what I was going to do with them. I stood under the ladder in the kitchen and shook the string over and over, hard as I could."

Thomas put his head down on his knees and laid his bandaged hands up over it. How humiliating.

But she wouldn't ever know it. He lifted his head indignantly. "I don't believe you! You can say it on a stack of Bibles. I don't believe you!"

"That's all right," she said. "It's more fun to believe it was a ghost. For me, too."

Thomas stared at her, trying to feel really angry. To his amazement he couldn't. He felt instead a certain amount of admiration. "You plain outtricked me," he said, to his own surprise.

She shrugged off his compliment, her face bright with another idea.

"But Guillermo is real," she said. "And there's one good thing about his coming to the store."

"There is?" He sat up straight, knowing suddenly what she meant. "We know for sure Guillermo hasn't found the treasure. That means it's probably still under the house."

"We'll start digging again tomorrow!" she cried.

"We're bound to find it!" Thomas felt certain.

They both fell silent then. Around them the sounds of the night buzzed, chirped, rattled, and whistled through the trees.

Thomas was not afraid. They were the familiar sounds he'd grown up with. Home sounds. And tonight every cricket whispered a promise.

▲215